JOY IS NOT HERSELF

JOY IS NOT HERSELF

Josephine Lee

Illustrated by Pat Marriott

Harcourt, Brace & World, Inc., New York

© 1962 by Josephine Lee
Illustrations © 1962 by Jonathan Cape Ltd.

First American edition, 1963
Library of Congress Catalog Card Number: 63-7898

Printed in the United States of America

To
Norman Gowing

CONTENTS

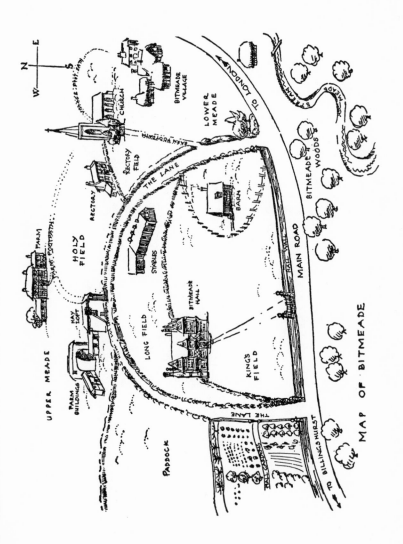

MAP OF BITMEADE

JOY IS NOT HERSELF

1

THE FIRST SIGNS

The day came when we could no longer pretend it was just another family joke. I was the first to feel fear, homely and familiar as the taste of bread and butter: there was no mistaking that feeling. The day itself was one of our ordinary days —the autumn half-term holiday—and we were going to Kensington Gardens. It was the usual weather, too, damp and drizzle, and a Monday—Father's busy day. While she was thinking of something else, we persuaded Mother to promise us a picnic in spite of the weather, but she emerged from her Monday trance to say that we were to be home by five o'clock to avoid the rush hour. As usual, we forgot the time until the bell began to ring, melancholy and impressive in the mist, making us feel as if the end of the world might come if we didn't hurry. We tried running down Exhibition Road, but we had to keep stopping for Melisande to catch up. The subway was crowded, but we pushed our way in. David and Peter were wedged somewhere in the middle, and Melisande and I were thrust against the doors.

Melisande had made a coronet of dead leaves, which she insisted on wearing. "Look the other way if you can't bear it," Mother would have advised. "She'll grow out of it if we take no notice." Taking no notice is what Mother's best at—

all very well for her—but Melisande's been like this ever since she was born, and ten years is a long time not to have grown out of it. However, I ignored Melisande and gazed at the two elderly gentlemen propped up close to us. They were solemn and neat and smooth—not a bit like Father.

Suddenly Melisande tapped one of them and said in her most penetrating voice, like the bell ringing out of the mist in the park: "Excuse me. Might I speak to you, sir?"

When Melisande is polite, it's like shaking hands with a snake.

"Would you mind telling me"—and she tapped him again, like a bird trying to break a large crumb with its beak—"if you're thinking at this minute of whether to cut down the old maple tree on the lawn of your garden in Sunningdale?"

He mopped his forehead with a very clean white handkerchief about as big as a sheet. His friend stopped trying to fold his newspaper into a long spill so that he could read it in the crush and stared at Melisande.

"Please don't mind my little sister," I began as usual, but the first gentleman interrupted.

"As a matter of fact," he replied in a voice that was almost a squeak, "I was. How the devil do you know, and who the devil are you?"

No one had ever said "how the devil" to Melisande before, and she took hold of my hand. It suddenly occurred to me that she wasn't altogether content to be "the other one" and that we ought to do something about it. People always call us "those three Montgomerys and the other one." The only

thing I could think of doing then was to get out at the next station. I tried to signal to David and Peter, but it was impossible, so I shoved Melisande onto the platform and hoped the two gentlemen wouldn't hear her crying: "But this isn't our station!"

While we waited for the next train, I tried taking Father's advice, since taking no notice was obviously the wrong treatment. I spoke to her kindly but firmly. "Look here, this sort of thing has got to stop. If you don't mind looking a fool, I do."

"Looking a fool!" she exclaimed. "But I didn't. I was right. I saw a picture of it in his head. I had to ask him. I had to find out if I could really do it."

She sounded very cocksure, but I didn't forget that she'd taken hold of my hand.

Whenever we complain about Melisande, Father always proves we're wrong with good reasons, and Mother defends her with common sense, so we usually try to cope with her on our own. But I didn't think we could manage this by ourselves.

There was toast and scrambled eggs for tea to make up for the wet picnic, and we took it up to my room. Melisande sat on the floor and fed her black cat with most of her egg and toast. I never saw anyone eat less. I wanted to make Peter and David agree that the time had come to take Father into our confidence, but I couldn't think of an excuse to get her out of the room. While I was wondering how I could possibly organize a private talk before Father came home, she picked up her cat and stood up.

"I'll go, if you want me to," she said, "but I know what you're going to talk about, so you might as well let me stay." She stared hard at my forehead, and I felt so queer that I turned my back on her. She laughed at me, but she went away.

"Which character out of what book does she think she is now?" Peter asked.

"She's not acting."

I told them what had happened on the subway. At first, they were sorry to have missed it.

"Come in useful, that sort of magic," said Peter. "I'll take her along to school just before exams to read the masters' minds."

"I don't think it's a nice sort of magic," I told him. "My head feels most peculiar, very light and thin, as if you could see through it."

"We always can," was his reply.

"You won't like it when she does it to you," I warned him.

"I don't like it now," David said, turning rather green. David's a bit squeamish. "It's gruesome," he added, with a shiver. You'd never think his father was a doctor.

After that, we didn't say much to each other, and as soon as we heard Father's key in the lock, we rushed downstairs. Mother took one look at us and produced some sherry. She poured a glass for him.

"Looks like a deputation," he said.

"It's Melisande," I began.

"It always is," said Mother.

"She says she can read other people's thoughts, that she sees pictures in their heads," I explained.

Father laughed. "Haven't you heard of telepathy?" he asked. "You're behind the times."

There was the good reason.

"Or coincidence?" Mother asked.

There was the common sense.

"Not to mention imagination."

"She isn't imagining. I was with her. On the subway, coming home this evening, she told a man what he was thinking, and she was right. She even knew where he lived. She's very pleased with herself."

"So would you be," said Mother.

I wanted to make them forget reason and common sense. I felt as if this were our last chance, as if the bell were ringing again and that we'd be left alone and shut in, surrounded by mist. I felt again that we must hurry to be safe.

"You can't let her go about doing that sort of thing, not to perfect strangers in crowded places."

"Bit of an ordeal for you?" Father asked very kindly.

"It's not that."

"Then what is it?" Mother asked.

"It's the other one."

Mother and Father looked at me blankly. I wanted to explain, but I couldn't put it into words. I looked helplessly at David. David, as his reports say, expresses his ideas fluently. He jumped off the stool by the stove, where he always sits for kitchen councils.

"Do you think she's a changeling?" he asked Father.

"Crikey!" Peter scoffed. "I didn't know you believed in fairies."

That started a tussle, of course. Mother calmly stepped over them, battling on the floor, as if they didn't exist, but Father raged. The trouble with Father's rages is their unexpectedness—no chance to prepare excuses or escape punishment.

"I won't have superstition!"

Down came his fist on the table, and over went the sherry.

"I spend all day listening to old wives' tales, and I don't want to come home to more. You know as well as I do that there's a rational and scientific explanation for every phenomenon, and if there isn't yet, there will be. Don't let me hear such nonsense again from any of you."

He put out his hand for his sherry and then looked at the upset glass in utter astonishment.

"What's a phenomenon?" David asked. (He never misses a new word.)

"Whatever do you want to know that for at this particular moment?"

"You just said it," David explained.

"Did I?" Father looked surprised.

"Melisande's a phenomenon," said Mother, "but don't tell her I said so."

"She's nothing of the sort," said Father, simmering. "It's your sympathy she needs, not your curiosity."

"Oh, we're sorry for her all right," Peter said, and I could tell he felt as I did. He wanted them to guess how worried we were; but adults, as he cynically remarked later, are only good at detecting falsehoods, not at guessing the truth. In his anxiety, he went too far.

"Rotten luck to look like something brought up from the bottom of a well and have a screw loose into the bargain," he added.

At that, Father erupted.

"I thought you were capable of taking part in a sensible discussion. If you prefer to behave like a silly boy, you can be treated like one and go straight to bed."

"Let's say no more about it," Mother intervened tactfully.

We didn't say any more about it. Instead of wishing we had a week's holiday, we were glad half-term was over and that we'd be back at school the next day. We knew now that we'd got to manage Melisande ourselves, but we were glad to put it off. Also, it was the season for horse chestnuts, which the boys all used in playing conkers. Peter and David didn't want to be convinced that "the other one" was evil until the conker season was over, because Melisande was a wonder at finding them. Peter's thirteen, and when next we went to gather conkers, he pretended he came to help David, who is only eleven; but of course he was just as keen on collecting them as the rest of us and stuck close to Melisande, to make sure of finding the most.

We went to the Gardens again on the first Saturday after half-term, but the chestnut trees had been plundered clean. There was a gang of boys throwing up pieces of deck chair, but they weren't even bringing down any empty burs. Melisande sauntered up and down the long line of horse chestnuts, just inside the gate by the flower beds, and came back to us with her hands full of beauties, perfect specimens, king conkers every one. The gang gathered around, and I hoped they wouldn't try to take the conkers. Normally, this isn't the sort of thing I worry about, but I remember the feeling of fear again and thinking that there weren't any grownups for miles—it was a cold, dank afternoon—and no sign of a keeper. But the boys just stood and stared at Melisande while she put the conkers in her pockets and said to us: "Let's go home. There aren't any more. I'm cold."

As we turned away, I said to her: "Why don't you give them some?"

"Are you afraid?" she asked.

I certainly was, and Peter and David didn't seem as ready as usual to make a fight of it. We tried to make her hurry, for the boys began to follow us, shouting and hurling bits of deck chair. Melisande looked back and stopped. She emptied the conkers out of her pockets onto the grass.

"There you are!" she called to the boys. Then she said to us: "Now, run!"

Without thinking, we did as she said, though we don't usually run away when we're afraid. We looked back when we got to the gate by the refreshment pavilion. The boys were searching in the grass where Melisande had dropped the conkers, scratching their heads, shrugging their shoulders, and staring after us. All the way home, Melisande smiled horribly to herself.

"How did she do it?" David asked.

"Goodness knows." I sighed.

"If anyone knows how Melisande does it, it isn't goodness," Peter observed.

All the same, even if she could conjure up two pocketfuls of conkers and then make them disappear and turn us into cowards, Melisande couldn't stop catching a cold on that autumn afternoon. She was in for one of her bad winters, Mother said, and, indeed, she was hardly ever able to go to school. Though Father stood around the bed for hours, he couldn't find anything really wrong with her. After Christmas, she recovered quite suddenly. And then it rained and rained for the rest of the holidays.

2

THE FIRST SPELL

We set about trying to think of something to do, though holiday boredom had never been a problem of ours until then. Mother brought Melisande up to my room.

"She's getting over the worst now," Mother said. "Company will be good for her."

"Over the worst!" Peter exclaimed when Mother had gone. "If you ask me, the worst is yet to come."

"It doesn't occur to Mother," David remarked, "that Melisande's company might not be good for us."

Melisande ignored our taunts. She sat staring out of the window at the rain falling like broken spears from the low sky. Suddenly I felt ashamed.

"Let's play an alphabet game," I suggested. "Come on, Melisande. You choose the first thing."

There was no reply, but I persevered. "What about rivers?"

"Enough wet everywhere already," Peter objected.

"She'll never think of anything," said David impatiently. (He always wins alphabet games.) "Let's have heroes and heroines."

Melisande turned from the window. She looked at me with the same expression she has when we let her choose her cake first.

"All right, Judith. I'll play."

But it was no good; for one thing, she could never remember the alphabet properly.

At the end of the first week of her convalescence, we were on the verge of a quarrel the whole day, although she hadn't done or said much but just sat in my room with the black cat on her lap. It was almost time for tea on Friday when I threatened to chuck them all out.

"It is supposed to be *my* room," I said, though I'd never made a fuss about this privilege (one of the few advantages in being the oldest) until that dismal afternoon.

David got up and gazed out of the window.

"It's dark as midnight and dreary as a desert," he announced. Then he sighed. "I do wish we lived in the country instead of in a flat in the middle of London."

"So do I!" I echoed.

Rain in the country, we thought, would be exciting; we didn't know much about it then. We'd always known that living in the country was impossible for us, however much we wished it, because of Father's work. Until that afternoon, we'd been content to dream about it. Suddenly we all believed it could really happen, thought of ways to make it happen.

"We could ask Father to swop over to a country practice," Peter suggested.

"He's known some of his patients since before they were born. We can't ask him to start on a new lot now."

"Ill people are advised to leave London and go to live in

the country," David informed us. "They have to be rehabili-
tated."

"Look at us!" I answered. "We're like an advertisement for
After Taking Ovaltine."

"Except Melisande," Peter said. "She looks like Before."

Melisande is as pale as cream cheese and thin as a worm.
As well as being short-sighted, she's left-handed, round-
shouldered, and knock-kneed, and her toes turn in. Her fingers are long and white and bony, and her hair is long and
lank and black. She has to wear braces on her teeth and
pink-rimmed spectacles. So, if you've been imagining she's a
cross between the Lady of Shalott and La Belle Dame Sans
Merci, I'm sorry to disappoint you. We're so used to her being
ill that no one would think of going to live in the country
on her account.

"Father is sometimes a prey to influenza," David continued
hopefully, in his worst fluent style.

"Only in an epidemic, and he won't even go to bed, let
alone retire to the country."

"That leaves Mother to go into a decline," said Peter, and
we all laughed. It was like thinking of a rhinoceros with the
vapors. Melisande didn't laugh. She stood up and looked at
us with her dark look. That's what David calls it, but Father
always says: "If you're going to be sick, Melisande, look
sharp and get to a basin." The cat stood up, too. It didn't
have a name: it was known to everyone as Melisande's cat.
She found it by the river when we went to visit the Tower

one wet Sunday afternoon. It always ignored the rest of us and would allow only Melisande to feed it.

"Would you like a weekend cottage?" Melisande asked. "Would that do?" We stopped laughing.

"It's a sensible idea," answered Peter admiringly. "If we could ever afford it."

"I could arrange that," said Melisande.

"The devil you could!" answered Peter.

Melisande picked up her cat.

"Turn out the light and draw the curtains," she commanded, "and I'll cast a spell."

David looked at me beseechingly as Peter moved to draw the curtains and plunge us into darkness. I jumped up; I was going to fetch Mother.

"What will you say to her, Judith?" Melisande said to me. "She'll only tell you to humor me, as I'm under the weather." Then she paused, uncertain. "Under the weather," she repeated, half to herself. "If only it hadn't rained . . ."

I wasn't going to have any more of this. I marched across the room to switch on the light but tripped over something in the dark and fell headlong. I looked afterward to see what had been in the way, but there was nothing there.

Before I could get up, Melisande had begun the spell. First, she said the alphabet backward, terribly fast.

"No wonder she doesn't know it the right way round," Peter whispered.

Without pausing, she went on to count down from a hundred to nought, and then (it was finished before we could

interrupt) she recited the Lord's Prayer from end to beginning. I was too astounded to move now, but David switched on the light and rushed out of the room.

He defended himself later. "You didn't hear what I heard at the end of it. You didn't hear the owl hoot." It was no use our saying: "Just as if there could have been an owl flying up and down Victoria Street at teatime!"; he wouldn't admit he'd imagined it.

Melisande put down her cat and walked out of the room. The cat followed her.

"That's the sort of thing she practices by the hour when she's not at school," said Peter in his best offhand manner. I didn't bother to reply; he knew he hadn't convinced me or himself. I opened all the windows wide. Perhaps it would blow away.

The next morning, I knew it hadn't. Mother collapsed when she got up and had to go back to bed. She looked very pale, and every time she tried to get up, she fainted.

"It's ridiculous!" she protested. "I've never had a day's illness in my life."

The next day she admitted that a day's rest hadn't put her right and that she had a pain in her heart. On the third day, she was much worse. Father got a nurse, and a grand consultant came several times, but he couldn't give a name to Mother's strange and sudden disease. At the end of the week, we had to go back to school, Melisande as well. Each evening we came home to find that there was still no improvement, and Melisande went about smiling her horrible smile. Mother refused to be moved to the hospital, and finally Father called in the most eminent physician he could think of. Father discussed the case openly with us—there was no point in his trying to pretend it was nothing serious with all this going on.

As soon as the great man had gone, I made some tea, and we waited for Father to come and tell us his verdict.

"Seems to think it's stress," Father informed us.

"Thought that had something to do with poetry," said David, puzzled.

"It's the modern word for a nervous breakdown, more or less," Father told him. "We've got to try a new approach: change of scene, regular rest, and fresh air, so I'm going to look for a weekend cottage in the country."

We all, as one man, choked into our cups. Luckily, Father put it down to our being stunned by the idea. Mother's appetite began to come back, and she put on weight again. Father thought it was all due to the new treatment—even the idea was a tonic—and we didn't see how we could tell him about the spell. Things had gone too far, and in any case he'd had enough to worry him.

We read advertisements and wrote to agents, and Father pestered all his patients. He spent his next few Wednesday afternoons off going to look at things that might do, but there was always something not quite right—usually the price. It would have to be miles from anywhere and falling to pieces for us to be able to afford it.

We forgot all about Melisande and her spell on the night

that Father came home and from one look at his face we knew he'd found it. We all trooped into their bedroom, which was our general meeting place now, because Mother still had to spend a lot of time resting.

"I think this is going to be successful," Father said at once. "A friend of a friend of a patient knows a man who's got a big place down in Sussex. It's not even a village, but part of an off-the-beaten-track hamlet."

"What's it called?" I asked.

Father looked anxious for a moment.

"I've written it down somewhere."

We jigged up and down on the bed while he sorted out his wallet—empty envelopes, screwed-up prescription forms, old bills, and ticket stubs for the Royal Ballet. (Mother's very keen on opera. She wanted to call us Siegfried and Rudolph and Carmen, but Father put a stop to that, thank goodness. She had her way about Melisande, though.) At last Father found the page, torn out of the back of his visiting book, on which he'd written the precious name and address.

"Gilbert Ridley-Ward," he read out with some difficulty. "Bitmeade Hall, near Billingshurst, Sussex. I didn't mean it to be quite so far from London for weekends, but you'll be able to go down with Mother in the holidays as well."

"But you'll only be able to come every other weekend. I'd forgotten that," said Mother guiltily.

(Father and another doctor have an arrangement to look after each other's patients on alternate weekends and one afternoon a week so that they get some time off.)

"It's your rest cure," Father said. "Don't you worry about me. I'll practice looking after myself when you're not here, so that by the summer holidays, I'll be a perfect grass widower."

"What's it like, the cottage?" I asked.

"It's not really a cottage, but a converted barn." We whooped with delight.

"There's one big room, divided by a partition to make a living room and a place to keep the sink. That's all there is at the moment, but if we call that part the kitchen, it'll turn into one in no time."

I looked at Melisande, half expecting her to wave a magic wand. I didn't like to think that we were getting so much pleasure from a spell that had made Mother dangerously ill, so I thrust it all to the back of my mind.

"There's a ladder leading from the kitchen up to a loft, where you'll all sleep."

At this news, David turned a somersault and fell off the bed.

"Mother and I will be comfortable in the main room. Furnishing's going to be a problem for some time. There won't be much money to spare."

We were ready to sleep naked on the floor and eat off newspaper.

"Can we go this weekend?"

"I haven't even seen it yet—only spoken to Mr. Ridley-Ward on the telephone. There's a farm belonging to the Hall, but that's rented out. Ridley-Ward's not a farmer but comes up to town several times a week to direct companies, I believe. I'm to go on Wednesday. He's driving me down in his Bentley after lunch at his club."

We gasped with envy.

"I'll come back by train, and I'll probably be fairly late, so no waiting up."

"Don't decide you don't like him, will you?" Mother pleaded.

"He can't help having a luxurious limousine and a stately home," David added.

"You know how tolerant I am!" was Father's indignant reply.

First thing on Thursday morning, Mother came rushing upstairs, calling out: "It's all right. We've got it. We're going this weekend. Mr. Ridley-Ward's being awfully helpful and has given us a table and some chairs and lent us a couple of primus stoves. There's water and a proper lavatory, but no gas or electricity. We'll have to get an oil stove and some oil lamps, but candles will do for now, and I can cook on the fire as well. We'll take camp beds for you and that old sofa that turns into a bed for us. There's a patch of land round the barn already cultivated that I can have for my garden."

Mother had always wanted to find out if she had green fingers when it came to something bigger than a window box.

We followed her, still talking, downstairs and into their bedroom. Father asked the time and heaved a great sigh when we told him. Mother got back into bed, and we all climbed on after her.

"Mr. Ridley-Ward's being most kind," she continued. "After all, we're perfect strangers. There's no need for him to go to all this trouble."

"Is there a Mrs. Ridley-Ward?" I asked.

Father sneezed and yawned but finally sat up.

"I didn't meet her, because we went straight to the barn. I wanted to get things settled. I gather she doesn't get about much—got a weak constitution."

"Like Mother," said Peter, and she gave him a shove with her foot and knocked him off the end of the bed. She was quite back to her normal size and color by now.

"Any children?" David wanted to know.

"A girl, a bit older than Judith—fifteen, I think he said. Didn't see her either. She's enormously looking forward to your being there at weekends. She's an only child, and the place is very isolated. Can't be much fun having a semi-invalid for a mother."

When Father said this, I glared at Melisande, but she only smiled her horrible smile.

"Good thing the girl's got her own interest," Father went on. "She's tremendously keen on riding. Mr. Ridley-Ward said she'd love to teach you all. You can have your first lesson this weekend."

There was an uneasy silence while Father waited for our shrieks of delight. He looked at us rather nervously, more like Mother, and waited for someone to explain. Someone meant me, as usual.

"I'd thought of getting details for my first map—I'm planning a series."

(Cartography, as David tells me to call it, began as a hobby and is now my mania.)

"There will be paths and tracks where it won't be possible to take a horse."

Peter was quick to follow on with his good reason.

"I've been saving up for a tent. I've practically got enough after doing that paper round. If Mr. Ridley-Ward's going to let us make free with his land, I can learn to camp on different sites and in all weathers. I'll get all the experience I need for going abroad with the school party. You said I could go as soon as I was able to look after myself and my equipment."

We all knew why David wasn't very keen to learn to ride.

"I can't very well collect beetles from the top of a horse," he protested.

"I don't think you talk about the top of a horse," Father said vaguely. "Anyway, it will all depend on the girl. She might take one look at you and change her mind."

"And then you'll be sorry," Mother declared. "I'm sure once you get a taste for riding, you'll become mad about it. Everyone does."

"Girls do," Peter corrected her.

"I don't want to *force* anyone," Father interrupted, and we knew we'd have to be cooperative, that this was why

Mr. Ridley-Ward had been so helpful. We slid off the bed but stopped at the door when Melisande began to speak.

"I'd like to learn to ride," she said.

It's very easy to forget that Melisande is our little sister as well as "the other one." She has a dream life, just like the rest of us: she imagines that she's a beautiful princess with golden hair, riding on a white palfrey. She could actually pretend she was on one of Mr. Ridley-Ward's ponies. I was all for encouraging Melisande's dream life—it made her more like a Montgomery.

"It would be good for her health," I said.

"Just the thing!" Mother agreed. "Ideal."

"The trouble is . . ." Father began, and we all looked nervously at each other. Melisande seemed miles away from us again. She might as well not have been in the room.

"The trouble is," Father tried again, "that Eleanor—I think that's her name—isn't used to small sisters. It's more a companion of her own age that she wants."

Melisande picked up her cat and walked out of the room. We followed her rather gloomily, but the gloom didn't last long. We spent that evening deciding what we'd take—what we could make do with and what we'd have to buy. Mother made a general list, and we each had our own personal list. At the top of hers, Melisande had written "cat."

"What about broomstick?" Peter whispered to me. "She could ride on that."

3

A FOE AND A FRIEND

Bitmeade Hall is in a very secluded part of Sussex. The village is so small that it hasn't a proper name, so they call it Bitmeade. A main road comes through the village from the town, and the Hall is about two miles from the village along the road. They call it a main road, but it's more like a lane, not even wide enough for buses, which only come as far as the village and then turn around and go back to the town. A little way out of the village, on the main road, there's a lane that winds off, passing our barn, the outbuildings and stables, the Hall farm cottages, and the Hall gardens. It joins the main road again beyond the Hall. I knew what to expect because I'd already studied a map. They call it a lane, but it's little more than a track, and Father would have missed it if I hadn't told him where to turn off. When he'd come in the Bentley, Mr. Ridley-Ward had driven up to the house, and they'd walked across fields to the barn. The lane makes a big semicircle off the road, and it seemed ages before I spotted, through a gap in the hedge and across a field on a little hill, the church that I'd been looking out for. I knew that the gate into our field was only a few yards farther along, on the other side of the lane. We could hardly wait for Father to stop the car, let alone to open the gate for him to drive through. We jumped out and over the gate, and there it was. Our barn!

It was roofed with tiles the color of stored apples, there were wooden steps up to the door, and it stood on stone mushrooms to keep out the damp. Inside, there was still a faint smell of hay and corn and sacks and wood smoke. Mr. Ridley-Ward had been as good as his word, and there was a big old kitchen table, some garden wicker chairs, and two benches. When we'd added our things—the sofa that turned into a bed, a few cushions, an old rug, some books—and pinned up on the wall several of David's paintings and my maps, it began to look like our dream come true. I tried not to remember that we had Melisande to thank. She went off with her cat. They had to get the feel of the place, she said. By the time she came back, we'd made up our camp beds in the loft and Mother had produced some supper. We were all to go to bed early. Up the ladder and into our loft, where we could hear birds twittering and mice rustling, was the end of a perfect day and the beginning of a perfect life.

The ceiling of the barn, between the loft and the room below, was heavy and beamed, and Mother had hung a thick curtain over the partition to keep out the draft. We talked for a long time, and there were no calls of "Be quiet," "Time to go to sleep." They couldn't hear us. Melisande's cat wasn't interested in the bird and mice noises. It curled up on the end of her camp bed and went to sleep.

"My cat feels quite at home here," she announced as she

rolled herself up in her blankets. "We think the place is safe enough. It will depend on the people."

Next morning, Melisande and her cat didn't have to go on a prowl to get the feel of the people. Soon after breakfast there was a sound of horses' hoofs along the lane and a voice calling "Cooee!" We ran out to the gate to meet Eleanor. She stopped her pony very expertly and made it stand quite still. She was very smart for riding in the country, more like one of the procession we see every Sunday morning coming up Queen's Gate and going along the Row. She seemed very pleased to see us, and we certainly admired the way she handled the pony. We felt ourselves becoming keen to learn at the mere sight of her skill, as Mother had forecast. We all patted the pony and it didn't seem to mind, and Eleanor was delighted with our open admiration.

"Can you come up now for your lesson?" she asked.

"Fairly soon," I answered. "We've one or two things to do."

"D'you have to help?" she asked. "What a bore! Why don't you get a woman from the farm cottages? I'll ask Papa to get someone for you."

"Will it cost much?" I asked nervously.

"Haven't a clue. Is it important?"

"Oh, no, not in the least," Peter said airily, and David and I stared at him. "It's more for our character that we're made to help."

"Oh, I see," said Eleanor. "Papa said he thought your father was a bit of a crank. But don't be long."

It was a command rather than a request. "Judith can have Sherry; that's my other pony. Two of my friends who are away at boarding school say I can borrow Ginger and Bismarck. They're only too glad for them to be exercised. David can have Ginger, and Bismarck will be just right for Peter."

So far, Eleanor had ignored Melisande. Now she suddenly turned her pony and came alongside me.

"I see you've brought your scarecrow," she said, pointing her whip at Melisande.

I knew we had to be nice to Eleanor, that getting the barn so cheaply was a kind of bribe. I frowned Peter into unwilling silence.

"She's very keen to learn to ride," I said. "She's the keenest of all of us. We could take turns on your other pony."

"Not on your life!" Eleanor replied. "One look at her, and Sherry would bolt to Billingshurst."

Melisande didn't say a word but put out her hand to pat the pony. It gave a terrified neigh and shied away.

"See what I mean!" cried Eleanor.

The pony began to cavort up and down the lane, rearing and snorting, but Eleanor showed no signs of nervousness, although in the end she had to jump off. She led the pony back to us, tapping it lightly with her whip and muttering: "Quiet, Sultan, quiet, you brute."

"Enough to frighten an elephant," she said, glaring at Melisande. Then she turned to me. "Sherry's not nearly as high-spirited as Sultan," she reassured me. "Oh, do come now! I'm sure your father wouldn't mind this once. I'll take you on a leading rein, and we can go and collect Ginger and Bismarck."

We all looked at Melisande without moving.

"Oh, come on," said Eleanor impatiently. "We don't want any kids. We don't want her."

I think Father must have overheard some of this because he suddenly came up to the gate and told Melisande that her cat seemed afraid to come down the ladder from the loft. She shot off to the rescue, and Father nodded to us to go with Eleanor. I was allowed to lead Sultan back to the stables, and he came along docilely enough with me. She began to instruct us at once, telling us the names of all the parts of the harness as we went along, and we soon became absorbed and forgot about Melisande. Eleanor was a first-class teacher and had us all saddling and unsaddling and trotting around the paddock by the end of the morning.

"That will do for the first go," she said, "or you'll be in agony. You can have another lesson tomorrow."

She came as far as the gate to our field—though when David called it that, she was quick to remind him that it all belonged to her father and that eventually it would all belong to her. Before we had time to look suitably impressed, a curious procession came from the gap in the hedge of the rectory field and advanced up our lane, I mean Mr. Ridley-Ward's lane. First came Melisande, then her cat, followed by an enormous old sheep dog that looked as if it had been knitted, and, last of all, an old man in a black clerical hat, a black suit so old it shone green in the sunlight, and galoshes, though it was a dry day. We all began to laugh as they came toward us.

"It's one of her familiars," Peter whispered to me. "A hobgoblin in disguise, I expect. Now we'll have two of them to tackle."

"That," said Eleanor between giggles, "is our rector, the Reverend Tobias Cricklemore, commonly known as Old Sycamore, and his dog Bruno, because it's more like a bear. You ought to go to church to hear one of the old boy's famous sermons—he talks to himself like a piccolo out of tune, Mama says. He's come to call on your parents, I expect. Papa says he's a stickler for duty, in spite of his years and being bent double with rheumatism in the winter. He's got a fierce old housekeeper who mounts guard over him, and he spends most of his time growing flowers. I think he's got a collection of animals, too, but only a privileged few are allowed to see them."

"I suppose that includes you?" Peter asked, but Eleanor was suddenly deaf.

The strange quartet had reached our gate.

"One fright is enough for Sultan," she said, and galloped off.

We all shook hands with the Reverend Tobias Crickle-more, and then we all shook hands with Bruno. Before we could say more than "How do you do," Old Sycamore was on his hands and knees in the garden, examining one of Mother's plants—she'd been hard at work all the morning. Melisande and the cat and the dog stood in a row beside him. We looked at each other and grinned and went into the barn to tell Mother and Father they had a visitor. They came out, and in a second Mother was on her hands and knees beside Old Sycamore.

"How did you get on?" Father asked us while Mother and the rector rubbed leaves between their fingers and picked up handfuls of soil and showed them to each other. "I hope Eleanor provided you with hats?"

"Eleanor says we're all very good pupils but that I'm the best," I announced proudly.

"I said it was for girls," Peter muttered.

"You must buy Melisande a riding hat so that she can join in," I told Father. "Eleanor found some old ones for us but says there's nothing for Melisande."

"They're fairly expensive," Father said doubtfully.

"There's our famous secondhand shop," said Mother, who had gotten up and was helping Old Sycamore to stand up straight, bending him this way and that as if he were a folding ruler. Melisande never minded wearing castoffs. It always seemed as if she were dressed in a long, ragged gown and going barefoot anyway, even in her school uniform.

"It doesn't matter any more," Melisande said. "I don't want a riding hat. I'm going with Mr. Cricklemore to see his animals. And, after that, when he's had his nap, we're going to watch some birds."

"Quite right, just so. If you'll allow her?" He bowed to Mother and Father as he asked them in a most courtly fashion.

We had a family powwow about Eleanor and Melisande as soon as Melisande went off to the rectory. Father explained that he was afraid Eleanor was a natural bully.

"And Melisande," he added, "is obviously doomed to bring out the worst in any bully."

"Just keep them apart," said Mother, "and everything will be all right."

Mother's advice is always hopeless, but before we could tell her so, Eleanor came in. I suppose it would be silly to knock on the door of a barn in the middle of a field miles from anywhere, especially your own barn (for we were only renting it), but we thought she might have given us some warning. That was the last time Father allowed us to discuss the question of Eleanor and Melisande. We told Eleanor that Melisande had gone to see the rector's jealously guarded animals, but it was no triumph.

"She'll certainly be on the wrong side of the bars," was her comment.

I took a deep breath and filled my lungs with tolerance, but Peter and David rushed off to their tent and beetles.

"It's you she wants for a friend." Peter justified himself later. "Can't go about with a gang of girls all day."

I knew it was fair, but justice always seems to mean that the oldest of the family is landed with the unpleasant things. As it happened, however, the first weekend was altogether a success. I made Eleanor come with me on my first expedition and help make a rough chart of my map. I showed off a bit, and I could tell she was impressed, because she actually considered coming again next weekend, giving up some of her precious riding time. Gradually things sorted themselves out. Though we did find ourselves spending more and more time riding during the following weekends, there was always a brief interlude for our own interests. The biggest success of all was Old Sycamore. We didn't have to worry about Melisande at all. And then it rained.

4

TOUCH AND GO

It was one of Father's weekends at the barn, and he'd
brought some heavy medical books that Peter said would
make good doorstops.

"Actually," Father said, "I've brought them to read, and
I don't care if it rains all the time."

Mother was going to make some curtains for the downstairs window because of the moths that came in at night.
(She doesn't share David's enthusiasm for insect life.) We
went up into our loft and watched the rain teeming down.
Mr. Ridley-Ward had had a proper window put in at the
far end of the loft, where there'd been a hole for hoisting up
the hay. The downstairs window and the door faced into our
field, toward the Hall, but from our loft window, we could
see across the lane and the rectory field. Melisande was very
miserable because she couldn't spend all the time with Old
Sycamore. The wet weather brought on his rheumatism, and
he had to sit in a cocoon of hot-water bottles and blankets
or else his limbs got stuck and he couldn't move an inch.

Eleanor soon appeared, and we came downstairs. She was
particularly pleased to see us that weekend because it was
much too wet for riding.

"Would you all come down to the stables and help me

clean tack," she, as usual, commanded rather than asked. On this occasion, however, we were only too glad to help. She hadn't expected Melisande to include herself, let alone her cat, but all she could say in front of Father was: "Cats don't like rain, you know."

Melisande didn't answer, and we watched Eleanor's expression change from disgust to astonishment when the cat arranged itself around Melisande's shoulder like a fur collar and she put her raincoat over the top of it, capewise. As soon as we were in the stables, on our own, Eleanor began to bully Melisande.

"She'd better do her share of the cleaning," she threatened, "now that she has come."

"She hasn't done her share of the riding," Peter pointed out, and that made Eleanor leave Melisande alone.

With the four of us working hard, we finished much too quickly; and still it rained and rained.

"Let's come into the old hayloft," said Eleanor. "It's not far up the lane."

We made a dash for it, forgetting Melisande, who can't run very fast, and she eventually climbed into the loft, driping wet and out of breath. This naturally amused Eleanor, and the atmosphere was consequently quite pleasant for a while. We each made ourselves a bed in the hay and pretended we were each in our own boat in a tempest, but Eleanor got bored very quickly.

"There's nothing to *do* here when I can't go riding," she complained.

We tried our stock of alphabet games; we asked her about birds and wild flowers and insect life; we sang rounds. But she would only play each game once, she giggled when it came to her turn to start a round, and Melisande had learned more from Old Sycamore in a month about country life than Eleanor had picked up in a lifetime. Eleanor, however, wasn't going to listen to her.

"We can read up all that stuff any day if we want to," she declared. "Let's think of something exciting. I know! Let's have a picnic lunch up here. I can scrounge anything from cook."

"We'll bring our share," I said.

"We'll have a feast!" cried Eleanor.

"It's a century at least until lunchtime," David reminded us rather dolefully.

"What shall we do until then?" Eleanor asked. She looked about for inspiration and suddenly pounced on Melisande, who had just begun to dry off in the hay.

"You think of something," she insisted. "It's your turn."

"We don't do things in turns in our family," Peter objected, but I gave him a warning nudge because Eleanor was getting quite angry.

"It's time she did something," Eleanor retorted. "She gives me the willies, sitting there staring like a stuffed owl."

She got up and jumped down very hard in the hay that Melisande had tucked around herself. The cat stalked away, and I envied it. I'd have given anything to have stalked off at that moment. Melisande got up, brushing the hay off quickly, so that Eleanor was smothered and began to cough. Peter foolishly laughed out loud, and that made Eleanor even more furious. I didn't like the way Melisande was looking at Eleanor, but she answered amiably enough.

"All right," she said. "I'll take my turn."

"Let's postpone your entertainment until after lunch," David suggested. He didn't like being reminded of owls.

"Pity to miss the chance," Melisande said.

"Chance of what?" I asked sharply.

"Chance to show off," Eleanor butted in, and Melisande began to smile. "It had better be fabulous," Eleanor threatened, "or else . . ."

"It'll be that all right," Peter muttered to me. "She couldn't have chosen a better word."

"It won't be anything of the sort," Melisande said to us, though she couldn't have heard what Peter whispered. "I'm going to do a scientific experiment."

"Not on me you're not," said Eleanor.

"I'm going to hypnotize you," Melisande announced, and Eleanor roared with laughter.

"I'd like to see you try," she gasped.

"I wouldn't," Peter said to me.

"Why don't you stop her?" David begged me.

"She can't get out of it now," Eleanor said to him.

"I wonder if I'll ever get out of it," Melisande murmured to herself. Then she paused and looked at me wistfully, and I remembered how she had been pleased when I had tried to make her come away from watching the rain and join in our game on the day she cast the first spell. But I didn't know what she wanted me to do, and I was too worried about what she was going to do to Eleanor to care very much. I was not only stupid but also scared.

Suddenly, Melisande sneered at me; the change in her expression was terrifying. David saw and rushed to put his head out of the hay-hoisting hold; I think he felt faint.

"Get back to your bed of hay," Melisande ordered Eleanor, and without a protest, Eleanor obeyed. Peter moved toward them, but I stood as fixed as the beams in the loft.

"Look here, Melisande," he began, and I knew he was trying what I had tried so unsuccessfully—Father's kind but firm treatment.

"Don't be a spoilsport," Eleanor said. She was as docile as a fly in a web. Peter and I looked hopelessly at each other.

Suddenly, David turned so quickly into the loft that he almost fell headlong over the ladder, sticking up from below.

"Hurrah!" he shouted. "It's stopped raining."

Peter and I rushed to the hay hold and leaned out. It was only a lull in the incessant downpour—black clouds were still piled in giant heaps over the land—but David was right. It had stopped raining. Eleanor jumped up from the hay.

"Now's our chance to get the provisions," she said. "See who can get back first." She came to look out as well. "We'll have to be quick, or it'll start again."

She was first down the ladder, and David dashed after her. Peter looked at me in a rather shamefaced way, hoping I

wouldn't refer to how frightened we'd both been. Melisande was sitting quite contentedly in the hay, stroking the cat, which had emerged from its hiding place.

"I think I'd better go and help David," he said. "You know what his idea of a picnic is—all buns and chocolate and jam. He'll never think of cheese straws and sausage rolls."

I put out my hand to stop him as he stepped to the ladder, for Melisande had stood up and was coming toward us, crying: "Don't go, don't all go."

Peter hesitated. "There isn't time now," he said to me, "to

go into it. Imagine what Eleanor would say if she came back and heard us talking about 'the other one.'" And he followed David.

"They're both afraid," said Melisande. So was I, but I did my best to conceal it from her. I had a feeling that our being afraid was making things devilish hard for Melisande. Then Eleanor's head appeared at the top of the ladder, and she pushed some interesting-looking packets into the loft. Melisande tugged at my sleeve.

"Make her like me," she whispered urgently.

"We'll do our best," I promised, "but you'll have to make an effort yourself."

Melisande groaned. "You haven't understood," she lamented. "It's easy for *me* to be kind to my enemies, but not for 'the other one.' " Then she added: "If only you knew what an effort I *have* been making! If only it hadn't rained!"

That was all Eleanor heard.

"It's started again," she announced. "Keep on the whole weekend, I should think."

Melisande moved away from me; the cat came and rubbed itself against her legs. Eleanor began to unwrap her parcels.

"Hope David and Peter aren't much longer," she said. "I'm hungry; and their stuff'll get wet through."

As she spoke, they came sprinting back, stopping at the bottom of the ladder to recover from their rush.

"Just in time," they called up. "It's teeming again."

Melisande gave a sharp sigh so like a hiss that for one moment I thought there must be a snake in the loft. I was relieved when David and Peter climbed up, even though I knew they were even more cowardly than I was.

"Mother expects we'll all get pneumonia," David announced.

"She's as bad as Old Sycamore," said Eleanor. "He'll never set foot outside the rectory when it rains, not even in an April shower."

"He has very bad rheumatism," Melisande retorted, indignantly but childishly.

"And he must be nearly a hundred." Peter backed her up in this ordinary mood.

"That reminds me," said Eleanor, sitting back on her heels, "it's his birthday next Saturday. Mama always makes me take him something. He gets very excited about his birthday—second childhood, I suppose. I never have a clue about what to get, though money's no object, of course. I've given him slippers and mufflers and hot-water-bottle covers and mittens and snuff boxes and books and a walking stick."

"I know what he wants. I know what he'd like," said Melisande. "I'll give him a present, too."

"Decent of you to let us know in time." I encouraged Eleanor.

"I know what I'll give him. He wants a special rose bush, one of those with the tiny yellow roses that your Father's got in the rose garden. He wants it to grow outside his library window. I'll get him that."

"He wants a climber then," said Eleanor. "It's not the same as Papa's standard. It'll be jolly expensive."

"I'll go without my pocket money for a year," vowed Melisande.

"It might be difficult to get," Eleanor continued. "I think they're rather rare. You don't even know what it's called."

"I'll find out," Melisande replied in her confident way, but she only sounded determined, not sinister.

5

THE BIRTHDAY PRESENT

When we returned to London, we offered to club together to buy the rose, but Melisande said she wanted it to be her own present, and Father agreed.

"After all," he said, "you others hardly know the rector."

It was a welcome change to hear ourselves called "Melisande and you others," so we accepted Father's suggestion that we should each make a birthday card and leave the rose to Melisande. I drew a little map of the village and the church, Peter made a stained-glass window out of bits of sticky paper, and David painted a chaffinch that looked real enough to fly off the paper. We finished our cards by Wednesday, but Father still hadn't been able to track down the right rose. Then Father suddenly remembered that a patient whose life he'd practically saved had a brother who was an expert on roses. The patient was delighted to be able to show her gratitude; the brother was only too pleased to help. He knew at once what was wanted from Melisande's description but showed her a picture to make sure, and on Friday morning he produced a cutting of the very rose. We decided this must be a stroke of good luck, because Father's memory is usually nonexistent and because Melisande was always most like our young sister and least like "the other one" when it was anything to do with Old Sycamore. Father was sorry it was his weekend at home and that he wouldn't be able to see for himself how pleased the rector would be. Melisande planned to get up at the crack of dawn on Saturday, to be the first to give a present, but then there was a stroke of bad luck.

"There seem to be spells and counterspells going on," Peter said to me. "It's like one of those infuriating games of noughts and crosses when no one ever wins."

Something went wrong with the car, so that we had to put off going down to Bitmeade until Saturday morning. It was time Father had a new car, but there never seemed to be enough money. We knew the barn was a luxury, now that Mother was perfectly well again, and we thought Father was very noble to manage with the old car. He had a special man at the garage who was always very quick at putting it right, and it was ready on Saturday morning, as he'd promised. We'd looked up trains and buses, though, because Melisande was determined to get to Bitmeade somehow. We persuaded Mother to forget Father's solemn warning and drive in her usual rash way, and we got there in record time. Mother dropped us at the gap in the hedge, and we raced across the rectory field as fast as we could go without knocking the plant about. We didn't have to stop for Melisande to catch up—she went over the field like a hare. We were to let her go in first and then put our cards in the letterbox and not wait.

We stopped at the gate of the rectory to get our breath

back, and we all saw it together. In a tub, standing under the library window, was a rose plant. It was well grown, big as a half standard, ready to be pinned to the wall for climbing, and, from the look of the tub and the red label tied to the stem, had obviously come from an expensive nursery. Of course, it was left to me to investigate. Melisande stood limp and lank as an old corn dolly, and Peter and David were too scared of the housekeeper dragon. I took the cutting from Melisande, in case it wasn't the same, but we knew it would be. I had a vague recollection of the name— Father's patient had written it down on a piece of paper that Father had lost—and when I saw it on the red tab, I knew this was the same rose. In the tub was a card and on the card was written: "A most happy birthday to our dear Rector from Eleanor Ridley-Ward." I couldn't tell Melisande this. I took the card back to them at the gate. When she read it, Melisande took her cutting from me and flung it as far as she could, back into the field. I wished she'd cry. I would have. We didn't know what in the world to do or to say. Suddenly the door of the rectory opened, and out of the porch came Old Sycamore. I knew that he must have been watching and listening from behind the library window.

He came to the gate, taking a long time, for his rheumatism was hardly better, though the sun was shining brightly enough that morning. I had the presence of mind to hand him my card and wish him a happy birthday, and Peter and David followed my lead. He thanked us most courteously and gave his little bow. He was very stiff and could hardly stand upright again after he'd bowed to us.

He turned to Melisande and said: "I missed you last week, my dear. Come along in. I've something special to show you."

"We'd better go," I said.

"Why?" asked David, but Peter gave him a kick.

"We haven't unloaded yet," I said. "Don't forget Mother's by herself."

"You run along; don't wait," said Old Sycamore, and Melisande gave him her arm and helped him totter back into the rectory.

As soon as we were in the field, Peter exploded.

"If she wants us to go riding, I shan't. I don't care what Father says. She's a beast, a perfect beast!"

There was no need for us to say how much we agreed. If it meant packing up and going straight back to London, we weren't going to let Eleanor get away with this. Unfortunately, our righteous indignation wasn't given the opportunity of expressing itself—David's phrase for letting off steam. When we got to our gate, Mother was standing there talking to two splendid horsemen. On closer inspection, they turned out to be Eleanor and her father. They were going out with hounds on the other side of Billingshurst and spending the night at the Master's house there, to rest the horses. Mrs. Ridley-Ward had already gone by car. Mr. Ridley-Ward got off his superb steed, as David called it: Paragon was its name. He wanted to look at some of Mother's gardening efforts that he'd noticed during the week. Mother was achieving quite a reputation as a horticulturalist. (David again!)

As Mr. Ridley-Ward finished his chat with Mother and came back to the horses, Peter stepped forward and put his hand on Paragon's flank. Eleanor, who was holding the reins, pulled away a bit, but Peter didn't move. I could tell he was going to tackle her and that he intended Mr. Ridley-Ward to know what had happened, but before he could say a word, Melisande appeared, hurtling through the gate like a jet-propelled rocket. She was carrying something white in her arms. She didn't see Mr. Ridley-Ward and dashed straight into him. She must have butted him hard in the stomach, but he didn't wince.

"Look!" cried Melisande. "Look what he's given me!"

It was a white guinea pig; we all crowded around enthusiastically.

"It's all white, pure white, white as a sail in the sunshine, white as a . . ." David declaimed, but no one was listening. We all tried to stroke the guinea pig at once, but it burrowed into Melisande's jersey. Mr. Ridley-Ward beckoned to Eleanor to get down and look, but she pretended not to see and began to fiddle with Sultan's straps and buckles.

Mr. Ridley-Ward smiled at Melisande and rubbed the guinea pig on the nose and said: "Jolly little fellow! Where does he come from?"

"Mr. Cricklemore asked me when my birthday was," Melisande explained breathlessly. "I told him it didn't come very

often, that I was born on Leap Year's Day. It's not leap year this year, he said, so you can have your birthday when you like. So I said I'd choose my birthday on the same day as his for this year, and he said that, in that case, I must have a present."

"Fishing," said Eleanor in a scornful voice, but no one took any notice.

"So he gave me this," Melisande continued rapturously, "and didn't mind a bit when I wanted to rush off at once to show everyone."

I'd never heard Melisande talk so much, but the white guinea pig was enough to loosen the tongue of a clam. It had the loveliest eyes and whiskers, the softest fur, and the silkiest nose.

"Eleanor can tell you how to look after the little chap—if it is a little chap?" said Mr. Ridley-Ward.

"Oh, yes, it's a boar. Mr. Cricklemore has given me a card with all his family history beautifully written out."

"The guinea pig's family history, I suppose you mean," said Peter, who had quite regained his usual lightheartedness.

"His mother's name was Ebony and his father's name was Jet, and it was a great surprise to them when he turned out all white."

Words poured out of Melisande, and we were too stunned to interrupt. I suppose Mr. Ridley-Ward thought it was her usual way of going on.

"Eleanor used to keep cavies," he said.

Eleanor only looked at her watch and muttered: "Ages ago. I've grown out of that." Then she let out Paragon's rein. "Do hurry, Papa," she said. "It's getting late."

Mr. Ridley-Ward turned away from us, and Eleanor began to wheel around on Sultan, but there was no one but me to watch. The others were clustered around Melisande and her guinea pig. I could tell by the way Eleanor swished her whip that she'd intended to ride off in style, leaving us openmouthed with admiration. Just as Mr. Ridley-Ward put his foot in the stirrup, she called out: "Anyway, what on earth will you do with a guinea pig in a flat in the middle of London?"

"Oh, dear," Mother said. "We didn't think of that. It can't be done."

Mr. Ridley-Ward gave Eleanor quite a cross look and didn't mount but came back to us.

"That's all right," he said, patting Melisande on the head. "Eleanor can look after it for you during the week, and you can take over at weekends and in the holidays. There are some old hutches near the stables. You boys can clean out one of them, scrub it with a solution of permanganate of potash crystals, mend the holes in the netting, and nail up the loose boards. I'm sure the rector will give you some bran or barley meal for the weekend, and I'll get in a supply for you on Monday. And I'm sure your mother won't mind if you take a few carrot tops. How's that?"

"Oh, thank you, thank you," Melisande cried, just like any overjoyed ten-year-old.

"Are you sure Eleanor won't mind?" Mother asked warily.

"She'll be delighted," said Mr. Ridley-Ward very firmly. "She practically lives in the stables, as you know, so it won't be any trouble."

Eleanor dug her knees into Sultan rather viciously, though he was perfectly docile that morning, and rode off without saying a word, so that Mr. Ridley-Ward had to gallop after her. Mother said we could all go down to the stables straight away and see about the hutch, and when it was ready, Melisande must go back to the rectory to borrow some fodder. Melisande let us each have a turn at carrying him until he got nervous at being handed about and hid himself again in her jersey.

"I hope it's going to have a name," said Peter, while he hammered and David scrubbed. "I refuse to go about referring to Melisande's guinea pig every time I want to talk about it. The cat's bad enough."

Melisande looked guilty. She had forgotten her cat, and it was nowhere to be seen. When we asked Mother, about it, she said: "Cats don't like guinea pigs."

It didn't appear for the rest of the weekend, and we thought we'd never see it again.

"Cats often do that," Mother told us, "when they come to live in the country. They go back to their wild state."

We had our own views about this, but we kept them quiet. A white guinea pig instead of a black cat seemed to us an inspired exchange.

"Of course he'll have a name," Melisande replied to Peter. "You're not to call him 'it.' He's got a name already."

"Oh, I dare say," scoffed Peter. "Some fantastic thing like Antarctica, I suppose, as it's all white. I mean 'he.' "

"That would be feminine," said David, in his maddeningly superior way. "It would have to be Antarcticus."

"Well, it isn't," said Melisande. "It's Snowy."

The ordinariness of it reduced us to total silence. Old Sycamore was certainly a godsend. We spent most of that weekend, as you can guess, with Snowy. It was restful to have the place to ourselves, too, not to have to be pandering to Eleanor all the time. We hoped there'd be a lot of going out with hounds from now on.

"I suppose Eleanor knew she was going off for the weekend," Peter said suspiciously.

"I don't think she's a coward." I tried to imitate Father, as usual, but it was very hard indeed to think of a good word for Eleanor.

It was Melisande who surprisingly said: "Let's forget it. After all, if it hadn't been for her spoiling my present, I'd never have got Snowy."

We hated going back to London and leaving Snowy, but he seemed quite at home in his hutch. Peter and David had made a good job of it. We didn't see Eleanor before we left, but Mother was sure Mr. Ridley-Ward would look after everything, as he'd promised. The intervening week had never seemed so long, though we kept telling Father the whole story and describing Snowy to him and reading up all we could find about the care of guinea pigs. Peter offered to buy a female when we read that it was cruel to keep a solitary guinea pig, but Melisande said we should have to consult Old Sycamore first, because he was very particular about marrying off his animals.

The journey down to Bitmeade the following Friday evening seemed to take twice as long as usual. When we arrived, we were surprised to find Mr. Ridley-Ward waiting at the gate of our field. He opened it to let us through and then asked if we minded if he spoke to Father alone.

We all guessed something dreadful had happened. Was he going to turn us out? Had we done something unforgivable?

It didn't take long for him to say what he had to say, and when Father came into the barn, his face had a very odd expression on it.

"I'm afraid . . ." he began, but he didn't get any further because Melisande suddenly flung herself at Mother, crying:

"It's Snowy. He's dead. She let him die. It's Snowy. I know it is."

Mother looked at Father over the top of Melisande's head, and he nodded.

"Mr. Ridley-Ward says he'll buy you another, just the same," Father said.

"Idiot!" hissed Peter, and Father didn't bother to scold him.

"Did it get ill?" I asked disbelievingly. We'd read that cavies were very hardy.

"No, I'm afraid . . ." Father stopped to blow his nose, and then he tried again. "At least Mr. Ridley-Ward told the truth: he could have pretended that it was ill."

"It's Eleanor. It's Eleanor," Melisande insisted, with her head pressed into Mother's lap. But she wasn't crying.

"I'm sorry to say that it is," Father replied. "Mr. Ridley-Ward's even sorrier, and he says she's too upset and ashamed to come and tell you herself, though he would have wished her to."

"Thought you said she wasn't a coward," Peter muttered angrily at me.

"She forgot to feed it. Mr. Ridley-Ward doesn't go into the stables where Eleanor keeps her ponies, where the hutch is. He remembered to ask Mrs. Ridley-Ward to get some bran and meal when she went into the town, and then forgot about the guinea pig until we were coming this evening. Mrs. Ridley-Ward remembered to buy the stuff, but it got left in the back of the brake they use for big shopping. There seems to have been a general misunderstanding."

"But Eleanor couldn't have forgotten," Peter insisted. "She must have passed the hutch twenty times a day."

"When Mr. Ridley-Ward remembered about it and asked Eleanor this evening how it was getting on, Eleanor was thunderstruck, he said. They went together to look, and of course the poor thing had starved to death."

"If Eleanor pretends she forgot, then she's a liar," Peter announced.

"As well as a murderer," David added.

"That's enough," said Father. "I won't have that." But he was very halfhearted and not really paying attention to them at all. "Mr. Ridley-Ward's going into the town first thing in the morning to buy you another," Father told Melisande, but there was no response.

"Would you like to go with him?" Mother tried, but Melisande furiously shook her head.

"I'll go and tell him she doesn't want it, save him the trouble," Peter volunteered. "And if I happen to meet Eleanor . . ."

Father looked helplessly at Melisande, but Mother suddenly began to notice us.

"You'd better go with him, Judith dear," she said. She knew I was just as likely to want to punch Eleanor on the nose, and I knew this was her way of putting me on my honor. Sometimes I'd give anything not to be the oldest.

As we turned to go, Father settled the matter by saying: "Whatever your private opinions are, you'll accept Mr. Ridley-Ward's word. He's behaving very decently. It's the least you can do."

"I'll put Melisande to bed with a nice hot drink while you've gone, and it won't seem nearly so dreadful in the morning," said Mother hopefully. "It'll all blow over."

Melisande suddenly stood up very straight.

"I'm not going to bed," she announced. Peter and I stayed to see what would happen next. "I'm going to see Mr. Cricklemore."

"It's getting dark," said Mother. "You can go and tell him all about it tomorrow. Do you good to talk about it when you don't feel so upset."

"David can come with me," said Melisande. "But I'm not afraid of the dark."

As she said this, we three looked at each other. It was a flash of "the other one" that we'd almost forgotten since

Old Sycamore had appeared on the scene. We were those three Montgomerys and "the other one" again.

"You can both go to bed," said Father.

David, as he would have said himself, obeyed this injunction with alacrity, but Melisande didn't move.

"I've got to go now. I've got to go!" she cried.

Father took her by the hand firmly.

"Off up to the Hall with you two—perhaps it will come better from you—but don't be long and don't be tactless."

We knew how David would be feeling, so we ran all the way there and back; we wouldn't have wished our worst enemy to be alone with Melisande for long that night.

6

THE NEXT SPELL

By the next morning, Melisande was more like "the other one" than ever before. She refused to go and see Old Sycamore and said she was going on a hunt for her cat. Eleanor kept well out of our way. She had a good excuse: she was going to a riding camp in the summer holidays, which weren't far off now. At the end of the camp, there was to be a gymkhana, in which she intended to carry off all the most important rosettes and cups. She sent a message to say that there'd be no riding for us until after the camp, as she would be using all the ponies in turn for practice so as not to overtire them; and in any case, her friends, who were going to the camp as well, would soon be home from boarding school and would want Ginger and Bismarck. We missed the riding —and the ponies—but the less we saw of Eleanor, the better; and we were glad not to have to go up to the stables and be reminded of Snowy.

We could ride reasonably well now, and Father thought, if we had a cheap holiday in the barn that summer, we might save enough for our own pony by the autumn. Mr. Ridley-Ward found us a bargain every other day; he was most anxious to make up for the loss of Snowy.

When Peter and I went up to the Hall on the fatal night,

he'd been very upset, especially as it had been his idea in the first place, and he'd quite understood about Melisande not wanting another guinea pig.

"If there's anything I—or Eleanor—can do for Melisande, please let me know," he said.

"There is something," Peter replied. "Melisande badly wants to learn to ride, but there never seems to be a chance for her."

It was the nearest we ever got to telling tales about Eleanor, and I blushed for shame in the dark, but Mr. Ridley-Ward took the hint.

"After the riding camp," he promised, "I'll borrow a very quiet pony from a friend for Melisande, and then there'll be no argument."

We could tell he meant it, but when we told Melisande, she didn't seem at all excited. Mother thought she must be sickening with something, she was so uninterested. After all, it had been her dearest wish to learn to ride ever since we came to the barn. All she said was: "*After* the riding camp?"

We weren't sure if the "*After*" had any sinister meaning, but we were too glad to be doing what we really liked doing in the country to think much about it. And, at the very beginning of the holidays, Melisande did have one of her summer colds—which explained everything, as far as Mother was concerned. She sat about having headaches and nosebleeds, and Mother kept her in the garden. Father said there was a lot of German measles about that summer, and no one could remember if Melisande had had it or not, so they thought it best to keep her isolated, especially as Eleanor's friends had arrived. Their whole lives centered on the riding camp and practicing for the gymkhana, and Eleanor ignored our existence. We were too relieved to be hurt, but we wondered why Mr. Ridley-Ward didn't send Eleanor to a boarding school so that she could always be with her friends.

"They did try it once for a year," Father told us, "but Eleanor was very unhappy. She missed the ponies, of course, and away from home, the other girls bullied her. So she soon came back."

"Poor little thing!" said Peter, but Father won't have sarcasm, so we didn't make any more obvious comments.

The riding camp was due to begin at the end of the first week of our summer holidays and would continue for three weeks. Father was coming for the first fortnight of that time, and we planned to make it the best summer holiday we'd ever had.

On the Friday we had a great tidy-up, to make a proper welcome, and Mother cooked practically all day. We could hear Eleanor and her friends shouting distantly in the paddock; the girl who was going to borrow Sherry had arrived, and they were all having a last session. The horse boxes were coming on Saturday to take the ponies on to the camping place, and Mr. Ridley-Ward was to drive the four girls and their gear to the camp on Monday morning. Miss Pelham, the pony-club secretary, was already at the camp with some other adults, getting things ready and waiting for the ponies. Girls were coming from all over the country; it was a great feat of organization, and there'd be keen competition for the gymkhana. Peter and David and I had been asked to stand by, in case there was any difficulty in getting the ponies into their boxes.

"Nice to know we're not quite forgotten," was Peter's bitter comment, but Mother said that we must go gracefully.

We were tired by Friday evening, after our very thorough scrubbing and polishing, and the ponies were going as early as possible in the morning. It wasn't until Mother suggested that we should have an early night that David noticed Melisande had disappeared.

"I said she could go and watch them jumping, if she kept out of the way," Mother said, suddenly remembering. "It's been rather dull for her this week. You'd better go up and fetch her, Judith."

"I'll help you look for her," Peter offered.

"She can't be far," Mother protested. "There's really no need for you both to go," but we pretended not to hear.

As we hastened up the lane to the stables, we could hear them calling to each other that it was time to come in, as it was getting too dark to see the jumps. There was no sign of Melisande, and we decided to go up to the paddock. We'd only gotten as far as the stables when we heard them coming.

"She surely can't be with them?" I said.

"Why not?" Peter suggested. "Perhaps we're getting worked up for nothing. Let's wait here."

We went up to the stable door, and Peter was just going

to open it when I pulled him by the arm and pointed. I didn't feel like speaking. On the door were chalked three triangles, and inside the triangles were the numbers three, seven, and nine. There were some other curious signs, Greek letters I think, and the figures and numbers and signs were enclosed in a circle. Under the circle an equation was drawn: $147 = 7^2 \times 3$.

"It's some code," said Peter. "They're just the sort of girls who have endless silly secrets."

"It's Melisande," I contradicted. "It's another spell."

Peter didn't argue; we both grabbed handfuls of grass and tried to rub it off. We could hear them coming down the lane now. I remembered the tack-cleaning rags in the stable, and we got to work with these at top speed and soon turned the whole design into a chalky, grassy mess. We stuffed the rags back and were just about to rush off, feeling pleased with our eleventh-hour rescue, when Melisande suddenly appeared from inside the stables. Peter thought he saw the cat, too, but he wasn't sure and it didn't come out.

"You're much too late," she said, and there was that same wistful note in her voice that I always heard when she thought I was on the verge of understanding and when I was always most bewildered by the contrasts in her behavior and her expressions. She made me think she half wished we'd come earlier—or that one half of her wished it. Peter didn't seem to be aware of any of this.

"I should jolly well think it is too late," he replied, trying to laugh it off, "much too late for little girls to be out."

"Midnight to cockcrow," Melisande said to him sourly. "That's my time. I thought you knew," and she disappeared down the lane.

We went quickly after her, and the ponies clattered into the stables as we hurried away. We couldn't catch up, though, and question her.

"She sees like an owl in the dark," I reminded him.

"Don't you mean a cat?"

"You've got cats on the brain."

We squabbled all the way back, and by the time we got to the barn, Melisande was in her nightgown, innocently drinking hot milk, and as soon as we went to bed, she fell asleep.

I didn't know what I expected to have happened by the morning, but everything seemed to be all right. Our help wasn't needed because the ponies were easily coaxed into the horse boxes and were driven off in good time. I feared they'd have an accident on the way, but I heard Eleanor telling the others, in the afternoon, that Miss Pelham had rung up to say the ponies had arrived safely.

I spent the day hanging about, watching and listening. Peter had decided to seize the opportunity to get back to his serious camping. David's beetlemania was on the wane, and Peter had agreed to let him help. They were going to do their own cooking and everything, all through the holidays. They spent the day in the tent—preparing, they said. Hiding, I called it. I was glad Father was coming the next day, even though we couldn't tell him about Melisande. It would be comforting to have him there if anything was going to go wrong.

Nothing had happened by Sunday morning, when we walked toward the village to meet him. We didn't have to wait long, and on our return Mother produced coffee and homemade rolls. Peter and David took one sniff and decided they'd abandon their cooking plans for the time being. It wasn't until we'd eaten every crumb that Mother remembered there was a message.

"Fancy forgetting a message after all these years!" she said. "I don't think you'll be overjoyed: it's not a very good start to your holiday. Mr. Ridley-Ward wants you to have a look at Eleanor. They've asked their own doctor, chap called Langport in the town, but he doesn't feel like dashing out on Sunday morning, as it's not urgent. They think she's got German measles, and they want you to confirm it, that's all. They're worried about the riding camp. It means she won't be able to go, of course, and they want to tell Miss Pelham."

"Who on earth's Miss Pelham?" Father asked.

"You know, the pony-club secretary. You've met her several times," Mother answered, but Father shook his head.

"Never heard of her," he maintained.

"Anyway," Mother continued, shrugging at our grins, "she's taking Eleanor and her friends as a team for the gymkhana, and she's counting on Eleanor to make sure they win all the prizes. Mr. Ridley-Ward can tell her when he takes the others; they'll be able to go if he does it tactfully."

"Oh, well, if that's all," Father said, "I'll go and put the poor child out of her anguish. She'll want to know one way or the other as soon as possible. What a shame!"

"Is German measles a serious disease?" David asked Mother as soon as Father had gone. He'd turned his usual green color, and I began to wish we hadn't told him about the stable door.

"It's all over in a week," she reassured him. "I hardly knew if you had it or not."

"Only a week?" asked Melisande.

"They won't let Eleanor go to the camp, under canvas and all that, even if German measles is very mild and only for a week," I said very quickly. The way Melisande had looked when she thought her spell might be ruined had made me remember that Mother might have died.

"I don't expect so," Mother replied. "Mrs. Ridley-Ward's a great fusser, and anyway, there'd be a riot if all those parents got to hear Eleanor wasn't out of quarantine. The others will have to keep quiet about it if they don't want to be sent home."

I felt Melisande relax, and I heaved a sigh of relief. It wasn't such a wicked spell, after all. She only wanted to prevent Eleanor's going to the camp. She didn't seem to have any more evil designs on her, and after the rose tree and Snowy, I didn't blame Melisande for wanting to get a bit of her own back. In fact, it turned out to be quite a good spell.

It was German measles, needless to say, and Mr. Ridley-Ward decided that, while Eleanor was laid up, we could have Sultan and that I could give Melisande some riding lessons. Miss Pelham was sending back the pony immediately —Eleanor didn't want him left at the camp for anyone to ride. We'd have to keep to the paddock, but Mr. Ridley-Ward thought I had the makings of a good horsewoman and that I was quite capable of passing on what Eleanor had taught me. He'd spoken to her about it, and she didn't mind at all because she knew we'd look after Sultan properly, according to her own instructions.

Father was nervous, as Sultan was the biggest and most excitable pony, and he always came to supervise the lessons, but much to his surprise, Melisande was very quick and confident. At the end of a week, Mr. Ridley-Ward came to see how she was getting on and was startled at the progress she'd made.

"We'll get Miss Pelham to let us have Tina the moment they come back from the camp," he promised. "Tina's a gentle little pony she keeps for the beginners at the pony club, where things are very slack during the long summer holidays."

Melisande could go out on Tina across country with us, he was sure of that. We'd be able to have all the ponies for the rest of the holidays, because Eleanor's friends were going away and he was taking Eleanor and her mother to France. At least, as Peter said rather bitterly, we were popular as grooms, but I remembered Melisande's thwarted look and I was prepared to sacrifice anything never to see it again.

"By the time Miss Pelham wants Tina back," Father said, "we might go into this question of our own pony."

"I've got my eye on one that would do very well for Melisande," Mr. Ridley-Ward said at once. "If she had a mount, perhaps you could all come to your first hunt. We have our own meet here in the autumn—it's quite an occasion. Eleanor's friends would be pleased to have Ginger and Bismarck taken out. They'll have gone back to boarding school by then—they always complain because they can't get home for the meet. I'm going to try to arrange it to coincide with their half-term next year, so they'll be delighted to have their ponies broken into the drill for them. It would be a red-letter day for Melisande. She'd be the youngest; if we killed, she'd be blooded."

I saw Father wince, but he said he'd be glad to see the pony, when Mr. Ridley-Ward had a moment to spare, with a view to buying it at the end of the summer.

Dr. Langport, the Ridley-Ward's doctor, wouldn't allow Eleanor out for another week, and Melisande and I became very fond of Sultan. Melisande used to take her turn at grooming, asking me not to watch. Once, I went back to the stables for something and could have sworn I saw the cat in Sultan's manger, but it might have been a trick of the light, because Melisande looked at me quite blankly when I asked her about it. Sultan grew attached to us, too, while we were on our own, and we were quite sad when Eleanor came to claim him back. Father said that we should keep away from Eleanor for another week. We'd all had German measles, but if Melisande caught it, she'd be bound to have it very badly, and he didn't want Mother to be bothered with nursing her in the holidays. Peter and David hadn't been seen for days, except when they came up to the barn to ask for water, as though we were complete strangers. Mother thought they were taking rather a lot of milk, and she'd missed one or two other things from the larder, but they said they weren't guilty and it must be the mice. I looked questioningly at Melisande, but she stared coldly back at me.

Father knew I was itching to get back to my maps.

"Why don't you go and see the rector?" he asked Melisande.

"I should have gone the night Snowy died. It's too late now."

"Nonsense," said Father, but I shook my head.

"Melisande is right," I told him. "We've heard that housekeeper telling people in the village shop that the rector gave his first all-white guinea pig to the doctor's youngest up at Bitmeade and she let it die. She called us 'they callous Londoners.' "

"Why didn't you speak up?" Mother asked. "Why didn't you say what had happened?"

"We weren't supposed to have heard." I excused my cowardice.

"We don't know what really happened, do we?" Father said.

"Peter would have spoken out," said Melisande, sounding very much like a little sister. "I wish Peter had been there."

"But why don't you go and explain?" Mother asked, puzzled.

Melisande drew back and hissed in her breath in the snakelike way.

"I'd rather not," she answered, and I thought she

sounded unhappy, rather than proud, but it was obviously my imagination, because Father laughed and said:

"You're as proud as Lucifer."

Melisande didn't even smile, and I felt the familiar onset of fear and resolved to haul Peter and David out of their tent. At times like that, I dreaded being alone with Melisande, especially as Mother and Father were so unaware of my terror. All Father said, before going back to London, was: "Well, don't mope: there's plenty to do here."

The best thing Mother could think of to amuse Melisande was to let her help with the weeding. The trouble was, she wouldn't destroy the weeds. One day she made an enormous garland of them and hung it on the door of Snowy's hutch, but Eleanor threw it away. We couldn't always be watching Melisande, and she kept sneaking off to the stables.

It was a great relief when Miss Pelham brought the others up to the Hall on their way back from the riding camp. Mr. Ridley-Ward invited us to tea with them to hear about the gymkhana. The others weren't a bad lot really if they could have thought about something else but horses for a second and if they hadn't all been under Eleanor's thumb.

We discovered there wouldn't be any more riding for any of us that summer, after all. Some cousins of one of the girls were coming to spend a holiday in her house while her family was away, and they would want all four ponies.

"In the circumstances," said Miss Pelham, "there's not much point in my bringing Tina over, is there?"

I knew that Melisande ought to have a lot more practice,

especially out of the paddock, before she would be ready
for the hunt, but I wasn't going to appear greedy with Miss
Pelham looking at me as if she were only obliging Mr.
Ridley-Ward and wouldn't bring Tina at all if she had her
way. I was glad Melisande hadn't been feeling well enough
to come to tea.

I stood up and made a speech. I've never done anything
of the kind before or since, and I went red all over, Peter
says.

"We wouldn't dream of asking you," I told Miss Pelham.
"We know that we've been exceptionally lucky to have had
the use of the ponies, and we're very grateful indeed." I
turned to the other girls. "We've never had a chance to
thank you properly, but I'd like to say how marvelous it's
been for us."

One of the girls—the most timid of them all, so I suppose
she felt for me in my embarrassment—said: "You're really
doing us a favor. Ginger's the laziest pony for miles around,
and it's a treat to have him exercised and kept up to the
mark. If you didn't have the ponies, they'd be sent down
to the pony club during term time for anyone to hack about
on."

Miss Pelham sniffed, and the timid girl suddenly realized
what she'd said and shrank back behind her tea and didn't
say another word.

"If that's how you feel," Miss Pelham boomed, glaring at
the poor girl, "it's lucky for you that Eleanor's here to teach
them. They owe everything to Eleanor, and it's entirely due

to her that you get your ponies back in such good condition." Then she glared at me. "And while you're making pretty speeches, what about a bouquet for Eleanor? You don't know how lucky you are, chance of a lifetime for you townees, to have someone like Eleanor to put you through your paces. Shocking loss, her not being at the gymkhana; set us back dreadfully."

We were well aware of what we owed to Eleanor, but this was neither the time nor the place to point out to Miss Pelham how much we were indebted against our will. We copied the timid girl and concentrated on our tea, but Miss Pelham was on the warpath. We gathered the pony club hadn't done very well in the gymkhana.

"I hear you're hunting with us in the autumn," she bellowed—her voice was the same, whether calling across a field or a teatable. "I suppose you'll take that for granted, too? It's a great privilege, I'd have you know, and I hope you realize it."

"If Melisande has a pony," I answered, "Mr. Ridley-Ward's invited us all to the meet."

"*If* Melisande has a pony!" Eleanor laughed. "This year, next year, some time, never. Jolly long time your father's taking to make up his mind to buy it. Anyone would think he knew something about ponies!"

Miss Pelham thought this was very witty. It hadn't occurred to me before that Eleanor didn't realize Father was only waiting until we could afford the pony. I suppose fifty pounds was pocket money to the Ridley-Wards, but it was a small fortune to us. We knew Father would have bought us all ponies long ago if it had been possible; and we knew he was going without things he badly needed for the surgery in order to scrape up enough to pay for this one. Peter said afterward that for one horrible moment he thought I was going to get up and make another speech, say all this to Miss Pelham and those girls. He'd gotten a cup ready to spill to cause a distraction.

We got away as soon as we could after tea and made a solemn pact that we wouldn't mention horses for the rest of the holidays. It was bliss when Eleanor and her friends went off to foreign parts. We felt our holidays were really beginning. Peter and David disappeared again. Mother sometimes met them in the village shop, getting in provisions, and the villagers thought they were all mad when they greeted each other like long-lost relations. I resigned myself to Melisande, as usual, and let her help with my maps. Her gift of knowing when we were near water was useful, at any rate. Life in the country began to seem more like our dream life. All the things we had planned to do before we had the barn were coming true at last. And then the summer holidays were over!

7

THE HUNT

When we got back to London and the term started, we vowed to let bygones be bygones and go down to Bitmeade at the weekend full of love for Eleanor and enthusiasm for the hunt. Eleanor's friends had gone back to boarding school when we returned for our first weekend after the holidays, and Ginger and Bismarck were in the stables waiting for us. There was no sign of Tina, but we didn't like to ask about this when Eleanor greeted us with: "Hasn't your father done anything about that pony for Melisande yet? He's been to look at it, Papa says."

Father hadn't said any more about the pony, and we hadn't asked. Perhaps it was going to cost more than he thought.

"I expect he's negotiating," said David rather grandly, but Eleanor only laughed at him.

"Hemming and hawing, I suppose you mean? Papa can't stand the way your father has to consider everything from A to Z before he makes up his mind."

This wasn't a good start, and I didn't improve matters by insisting that Melisande should share Sherry with me, so that she'd get some experience before the hunt. Mr. Ridley-Ward said it would be at the beginning of November; he was organizing things with the Huntmaster during the coming weeks. That gave Eleanor about six weekends to coach us, and by that time Melisande was bound to have her pony. We would be the only children out, Eleanor told us; of course she didn't regard herself as a child.

She didn't want to miss the chance of increasing her reputation by showing us off as her first pupils, so she agreed to my suggestion of sharing Sherry with Melisande. She had visions of her own riding school and had practically gotten her father to agree to let her leave school to start one as soon as she was sixteen. Our behavior at the hunt was going to be her first unofficial advertisement, and while we were anxious to help what we admitted was a very deserving cause, as well as to enjoy ourselves, we made the most of our strong position. Eleanor trained us all thoroughly—Melisande as well. There was no time for anything else. Mother said, by the state of our camp beds in the morning, we went hunting in our dreams every night, and Eleanor was certainly giving us as much stage fright as confidence.

"You won't let me down, will you?" she said, at the end of a weekend's hard drill. "You'll get yourselves properly rigged up?"

We hadn't thought of that. We'd all gotten our own hats by now—Father approved of Eleanor's being so strict with us about that. Eleanor gave me one of her old hacking jackets and some breeches and boots she'd grown out of; the boys didn't matter so much, she said. Father sold some medical books that he said he would never read, and our secondhand shop was as cooperative as ever. Eleanor had said we were to have a dress rehearsal on the Friday before the hunt, but in the end we were all fully equipped a fortnight beforehand. Mother thought we shouldn't leave showing ourselves to Eleanor until the last minute in case any alterations had to be made, and that we'd better be inspected right away.

Father was going with Mr. Ridley-Ward to get the pony during his next weekend at the barn, the weekend before the hunt, so that Melisande would have a chance to go out on her first. Mr. Ridley-Ward said she was exactly like Sherry and that Melisande would soon get used to her. Father had managed to arrange two free weekends running, so that he could be there for the hunt as well. We weren't worried about leaving the pony for Eleanor to look after during the week—we knew she'd be conscientious about that, even if it was Melisande's.

She was very pleased with us for being ready in such good time. She walked around us and looked us up and down, until Peter said he felt like a waxwork and Eleanor retorted that he looked like one, in the Chamber of Horrors. Remembering our armistice vow, we all guffawed at Eleanor's joke, but it didn't prevent her from laughing at Melisande.

"Perhaps if she had a pigtail . . ." she mused.

I obligingly plaited Melisande's hair, and David produced a rubber band to wind around the end.

"She looks like an orphan left on a doorstep, or a Chinese refugee," said Eleanor.

"Will it do?" Melisande asked her rather pathetically.

"I suppose it'll have to," she replied. "Perhaps they'll think you're some kind of mascot, like a regimental goat."

Peter had a job to swallow that insult. If it hadn't been Melisande herself who warningly tugged at his sleeve, I think he would have made a final break with Eleanor and riding and the hunt.

I quickly suggested that we ought to change into our weekend rags before we spoiled our hunting wardrobe.

"Next weekend, when you've got the pony, I'll take you out and have a look at the possible country," were Eleanor's parting words.

They were famous last words. During the week, the engine of the car finally gave out. It had been threatening for some time, and though the man at the garage did all he could, Father had to get a new engine. We knew he couldn't possibly manage without the car at that time of year, and we knew that a new engine meant no pony. There wouldn't be enough money to spare for both.

Father didn't wait for the weekend but wrote at once to Mr. Ridley-Ward's friend, apologizing, and to Mr. Ridley-Ward, explaining. It was just as well we'd had our dress rehearsal, because we couldn't go down the weekend before the hunt, as we'd arranged, as the car wasn't ready. Father didn't want us to be out with Eleanor without Melisande, so we stayed in London and tried to be specially nice to her and not mention that we could have gone by train.

"Why is she passively suffering?" David asked. "Why doesn't she cast a spell?"

"I'm not a fairy godmother," Melisande muttered. "You know what I am. Or at least what half of me is."

We didn't want to argue with Melisande about her halves, in case she did do something about it, because by this time we were terribly looking forward to our first hunt.

David wasn't quite so selfish. At least, that's what we believed when he offered to let Melisande ride Ginger, until we realized that he was thinking he'd be the youngest, if Melisande wasn't there, and that he might have to be blooded if the fox was killed. Father, however (according to David), frustrated his benevolence. It was all right for Melisande to ride about in the paddock on the big ponies, Father said, but she was on no account to go out on them. For a hunt, especially, she ought to have a mount she could properly control.

David persisted. "We'll ask if she can borrow Tina," he said. "There won't be a pony club meeting because Miss Pelham's coming to the hunt."

We all cheered loudly and clapped him on the back, but Father frowned.

"I did promise Mr. Ridley-Ward that I'd buy the pony from his friend. I don't think I can ask him to lend Tina, now that I've let him down."

Peter joined in now. "He wouldn't mind. He told us that

if there was ever anything he could do to make up for Snowy, we'd only to ask him."

I remembered how insistent he had been on that horrible night.

"I'll write to him," I said.

Melisande gazed imploringly at him, just like the baby of the family, but Father obviously didn't like the idea.

"We haven't ever *asked* for a favor—they've all been thrust upon us," Mother pointed out.

This unanimous pressure was too much for Father, and in the end he agreed.

Mr. Ridley-Ward replied at once. He'd been to see Miss Pelham, and of course it would be all right. He was stupid not to have thought of it himself. He was sorry we'd have to miss the weekend before the hunt, but he was sure Eleanor had gone over everything with us down to the last detail. He did hope the car would be ready in time for the next weekend, but if it wasn't, we were to let him know and he'd meet us at the station on Friday night. He was looking forward to seeing us all turn out.

Father was overcome, and we all renewed our vow to be Eleanor's slaves, if only for Mr. Ridley-Ward's sake.

The car was ready in time, but we had to drive slowly because of the new engine. It was later than usual by the time we arrived at the barn, and Father made us go straight to bed. He promised to wake us up early in the morning, so that we'd have plenty of time to help Eleanor feed and groom the ponies.

"And to feed and groom themselves," Mother pointed out.

She cooked a colossal breakfast to give us a good sendoff, and she'd made some sandwiches for our saddlebags, though Eleanor said there was often no time to eat them. Mother plaited Melisande's hair, and Father shook his head. It did make her glasses and the braces on her teeth much more prominent.

"It's only for the hunt," we told him.

"Thank goodness for that. Eleanor's idea, I suppose?"

When we were all ready, Father said that we looked like the richest County family for miles, and he only hoped our performance would live up to our appearance. He and Mother were going to come up to the Hall to see the hunt move off.

We rushed up to the stables. Eleanor was there, looking staggeringly swish in a new habit.

"There's not much to do," she said. "I guessed your father would make you have an early night, so I got everything ready. I don't want you to get tired before you start or to muck up your clothes."

Sultan and Sherry and Ginger and Bismarck certainly looked as sleek as washed cats. There was no sign of Tina, but it was still quite early, and we expected Miss Pelham would be bringing her from the pony-club stables. Before I could ask Eleanor about this, we heard a rider coming down the lane, and in a short time Miss Pelham hove into view. We've got to say "hove," David says, because she was mounted on a stallion that seemed as big as a liner and

moved as smoothly as one. He was as fine as Paragon, and
we knew without doubt that Miss Pelham would win honor
and glory for the pony club this day. But there was no sign
of Tina.

We waited while Miss Pelham dismounted, and I saw
David cross his fingers behind his back. She walked toward us and muttered something to Eleanor while she
eyed us up and down, grinning openly at Melisande. As
she turned away, I saw her wink at Eleanor. It was done
in a second, but Melisande saw too, and she turned as
white as Snowy had been. I put my arm around her, but she
swung away from me and turned her back on Eleanor and
Miss Pelham.

"Where's Tina?" It was David who asked.

"Hasn't Eleanor told you?" Miss Pelham said in a careless
kind of way. "I rang up last night. Tina's gone lame, I'm
afraid. Some beginner drove her too hard at the camp, and
she's suddenly cracked up. I was too busy to keep an eye
on everything, especially as Eleanor wasn't there. Eleanor's
my right hand—but of course you know that. Mind you're
a credit to her today. You'll be on your own; you realize that?"

It was an ominous reminder, and Melisande didn't miss it.
She turned back to me and smiled her most horrible smile.

"Eleanor won't want to lag behind with you—can't expect it, can you? So don't do anything foolish."

That was all Miss Pelham said. She didn't look at Melisande again, and she didn't say she was sorry. She just rode

away, calling out: "I'm going up to your father. He's in the long field with Paragon. You might as well go up to the house. The hounds will be here soon."

"Good-oh!" Eleanor called back, but when we were all alone together, she was uneasy. I was sure that she was feeling guilty.

"You'd better cut back to the barn and change your clothes," Eleanor ordered Melisande. "You'll look a bit silly, dressed up like that just to watch. You can come back with your father and mother."

"If you don't mind," I said, "I'll go with her. You take Sherry up to the Hall, and I'll come straight there."

I was determined to hand over Melisande to Father, and it was obvious to Eleanor that I didn't care if she did mind. Melisande saw what I was thinking, of course, and began to run. She took me by surprise and got a good start. She wasn't running in the direction of the barn. Peter flung Bismarck's reins at David and dashed away to head her off.

As he did so, a black shape sprang out of the stables and followed Melisande like an aimed arrow. It was the cat.

Peter and I were not deterred by this. We ran harder and managed to converge on Melisande, and I grabbed her by the arm. But she slithered like a serpent, and the cat got under our feet, and she broke away.

We kept on running, one on each side of her, and drove her in the direction of the barn. Luckily Mother was in the garden, and she came to the gate just in time to stop Melisande whizzing past. The cat disappeared so swiftly that Mother didn't notice it.

"Well, really," she said, while we got our breath back, "I should have thought you'd have more sense than to go tearing about like lunatics half an hour before you're due to start. What's the matter? Forgotten something?"

"It's Melisande," I gasped. "Tell Father, keep her quiet. She's very upset. She might . . ."

"They haven't brought Tina," Peter interrupted me. "She's gone lame—apparently."

Father had come out now, and he overheard this.

"That's enough," he said curtly to Peter. "I won't have rumors. You get back now—don't keep anyone waiting. Melisande shall come up with us." He took Melisande by the hand. "There will be other hunts," he said to her. "Your turn will come."

"Oh, yes," she agreed, in her cool, clear voice, "my turn will come," and she unclasped Father's hand and went into the barn.

We stood at the gate, undecided.

"You go and enjoy yourselves now," Mother advised. "Ride it out of your systems."

"Miss Pelham's only concern is for the horses," Father reminded us. "Even if Eleanor's done anything underhand, there's such a thing as discipline and consideration for the feelings of others."

"Even if!" Peter exclaimed. "She must have told Miss Pelham a pack of lies about Melisande to stop her bringing Tina after all Mr. Ridley-Ward said in his letter."

"That's enough," said Father sternly. "After all the time and trouble Eleanor's taken, you ought to be ashamed."

"They ought at least to give her the benefit of the doubt," Mother echoed.

There was no more to be said. We went down the lane to the road and up the road to the front of the Hall. As we drew nearer, we could hear the hounds, the horses, and the people, we could feel the excitement stretching out toward us, and we knew we would forget Melisande the moment we moved off with the rest.

8

THE LAST SPELL

Eleanor was very annoyed with us when we reached the Hall because she'd had to stay with David and help him keep Sherry and Bismarck quiet until we returned. The arrival of the hounds had made the ponies restless; they were as new to hunting as we were. Eleanor wanted to be with her father, on Paragon, and with Miss Pelham, on her great beast, giving herself airs in front of the onlookers. Some were on bicycles, so that they could follow the hunt as far as they could by the lanes. A few other riders and foot-followers and friends of the Ridley-Wards were all assembled on the lawn, immediately in front of the house.

It was a bright, clear morning. The sky seemed very far away and very clean. Everything showed up brilliantly in the space and light: the red (I mean pink) coats, the markings on the black and white hounds, the gray, brown, and dappled horses. The house, like painted scenery behind us, was a perfect setting. Parts of it were Elizabethan, Mr. Ridley-Ward had told Father.

Mrs. Ridley-Ward had come out on the lawn with her friends. She was wearing a fur coat, like an actress on a first night, fur boots, and a muff.

"There's Mama!" said Eleanor.

As soon as Peter and I were mounted, Eleanor began to move off, but she reined up again when I said: "I think your mother's coming to speak to us."

As Mrs. Ridley-Ward came up to us, Melisande unexpectedly appeared. She gave Sultan a wallop on his flank that made him fold back his ears and rear off his front legs. Mrs. Ridley-Ward retreated in alarm while Eleanor calmed him down.

Melisande had changed her clothes with a vengeance: her hair was hanging around her face like Ophelia just drowned, and she was wearing one of my old pullovers that reached down to her knees and hung over the ends of her fingers, and a pair of my cast-off dancing pumps that she used for slippers.

She stood next to Eleanor's mother and peered out at her from the curtain of hair. Mrs. Ridley-Ward retreated

even further. I was slightly reassured not to see the cat.

"Where are Mother and Father?" I asked. "You're supposed to keep out of the way of the horses; you know that."

"They're not here yet," said Peter, glancing around.

"Mother's cut her finger rather badly," said Melisande. "They're looking for something to do it up with. It's bleeding a lot. They won't be long, but it will give me time."

She dodged away from us, and she didn't go and stand with the other spectators.

"Good riddance," Eleanor muttered, but David moaned: "Oh dear!"

Peter and I looked at each other. Should we go after her? It was nearly time to move off, and Eleanor had told us to keep as still and quiet as possible beforehand. We didn't want to draw attention to ourselves, especially after Father's admonitions. In any case, Melisande was so quick that we lost sight of her in a second.

"Like a fox, just like a fox!" Mrs. Ridley-Ward exclaimed, staring after her. "I suppose that's your little sister?"

"I suppose so, too," Peter whispered to me. "I wish I knew for certain."

"I've heard so much about her," continued Mrs. Ridley-Ward. Then she turned to Eleanor and said, not bothering to lower her voice in case we heard, "I should think it's just as well that Tina *is* lame." She smiled at us. "You look splendid—to the manner born." She flattered us and went back to her friends.

Eleanor took her chance to join Miss Pelham, who was waving frantically to her to come forward.

"I hope we find," she said to David as she left us. "It'll be a great day for you."

David was nervous enough already, and this reminder of possibly being blooded thoroughly upset him. Peter didn't make him feel any better by saying: "I wonder *how* Mother cut her finger?"

"Oh, pipe down," David begged. (Slang is always a sign that he's not himself.) "Where's she got to? What's she up to?"

"She's there, with Mr. Ridley-Ward, among the horses," Peter said, pointing. "He's talking to her, telling her to get out of the way, I think. He's following her now, making sure she does as she's told, I expect. Here they come."

Mr. Ridley-Ward nodded at us in a briskly appreciative way.

"Look as if you've been hunting all your lives," he said. "Sorry about this sister of yours, but she's young yet. There's plenty of time." He looked around. "Mother and Father not here yet? They'll miss us if they're not careful."

We explained what had happened to delay them.

"You'd better go and stand over there, then," he ordered Melisande. "Don't come up among the horses any more now, there's a good girl."

"A good girl!" Peter whispered to me as Mr. Ridley-Ward returned to the other horsemen. "I don't know what she is, but it certainly isn't that."

As we trotted down the drive to join the rest, Melisande vanished as unexpectedly as she had appeared. Then David, looking anxiously around, saw Mother and Father. We waved to them in a restrained way, in case we weren't supposed to—like not owning your parents at school concerts and prize giving.

In a moment, we'd joined the tail end of the procession, feeling rather self-conscious but beginning to be excited. All the village had turned out by now, even Old Sycamore's housekeeper dragon, but there was no sign of the rector.

"He's bound to agree with Father," Peter said. "If he's disowned us because he thinks we let Snowy die, goodness knows what his views on fox hunting must be."

We could see the riders ahead of us gently trotting out of the drive now, the Master and the Huntsman, Mr. Ridley-Ward and the rest of the horsemen who were strangers to us. Some more riders joined them at the road.

As Eleanor and Miss Pelham followed, we saw them look down at Sultan's tail. All the horses had very fine tails, though Eleanor had told us that in her grandfather's day even the hunting horses were docked. Then Miss Pelham let Eleanor go forward and stooped as she did to pull something out of Sultan's tail. She showed it to Eleanor and they shrugged, and she threw it on the grass verge by the wall, and they were lost to view. When we turned out of the drive into the road, I looked on the grass to see what Miss Pelham had taken from Sultan's tail and thrown there. I told Peter to look.

"Sultan's always swishing his tail, even when there isn't a fly for miles. Probably got a bit of grass tangled in it," Peter said. "Only Miss Pelham and Eleanor would worry about a thing like that."

We saw what did indeed look like a bit of grass at first, and Peter began to laugh at me. As we looked closer, however, his laughter changed to a gasp of horror. It wasn't grass but a woven plait of deadly nightshade, ivy, bittersweet, white bryony and black bryony. We recognized them quickly enough. Before we even came to the barn, Father had taught us which were the poisonous plants and berries. It was undoubtedly Melisande's work.

"How did she manage to do it without being observed?" I said.

"Made herself invisible," Peter replied. "Or trained the cat!" Before I could tell him it was no laughing matter, the cavalcade began to canter, and we left the road.

There was no time for conversation. We rode across a field and alongside a wood. Melisande was forgotten while we waited in a fever of anticipation for the hounds to draw the wood. Her malice was driven from our minds by the sound of the horn, the cry of the Master, and the bay of hounds as they found a fox. The horn echoed over the countryside in the cold, unclouded morning, and we were away, galloping now. For all Father and Old Sycamore might preach, and for all I secretly agreed with them in cold blood, there was exhilaration in the feeling of being one with the other riders. There was satisfaction in watching the skill of the hounds and the experience of the hunts-man. There was a thrill in the knowledge that one's own pony was doing the right thing, in the feel of confidence and alertness. I hoped we would be able to keep up, that we would remember, without thinking, everything that Eleanor had taught us. Even David, galloping now beside me on Ginger, cried out: "Poor old Melisande!"

We had a good hunt, without hounds killing, and it was late in the afternoon when Eleanor was thrown. No one saw it happen. She was found lying in the middle of a field, with Sultan grazing nearby. When we three arrived, her father was standing over her, the rest of the field having galloped on.

Our excitement went out as if a shovel of wet ashes had been put on a roaring fire. Mr. Ridley-Ward's eyes were watering, and for one wild moment we believed he was crying. But he pointed to Sultan and said: "Don't know what's the matter with the pony—gave me a great slash with his tail when I knelt down to look at Eleanor—nearly blinded me."

He didn't seem to have the faintest idea what to do and stared at us as if he were in a trance.

"If you tell me where we are—the nearest approach to Bitmeade by road—I'll go for Father," I suggested. "I don't think we ought to move her. Father can drive here and tell you how she ought to be lifted to the car, and you can take her straight on to the cottage hospital in the town."

He hardly heard what I was saying. He simply gazed from Eleanor to Sultan and shrugged helplessly.

"Quicker than trying to find a telephone for an ambulance out here," Peter added.

David joined in. "Judith's got a good sense of direction. We'll get there in no time." He was determined not to be left behind.

Mr. Ridley-Ward pointed vaguely in what he thought was the direction of Bitmeade Hall, but I knew from what was left of the sun that it couldn't be. By now, Miss Pelham and one or two of the others were galloping back to see what had happened, and we didn't waste any more time.

"How they brought the good news from Aix to Ghent," Peter quoted mournfully as we rode.

"It was Ghent to Aix," David contradicted, but more from force of habit than an urge to triumph.

Fear made us ride like—no, no, not like the devil! Luckily, we met Father in the village. He'd driven down to the shop to buy things for the great feast we were to have had on our return.

He made us all feel calm and collected at once. Peter was to ride to the barn and tell Mother to go up to the Hall and prepare Mrs. Ridley-Ward for the shock. Mother's had a lifetime of experience at preparing people for shocks of that kind. I was to telephone Dr. Langport from the village shop and tell him to be at the cottage hospital to wait for Eleanor's arrival. If I couldn't get him, I was to ring up the doctor in charge at the hospital and explain everything. David was to go to bed.

We looked at David: he really did look ghastly. As Father drove off, we noticed all the customers in the shop had come outside to listen. Peter galloped off, tired as he was, to make sure Mother got to Mrs. Ridley-Ward before the rumors, and David came into the shop with me. It was practically closing time.

"It's saved a lot of valuable time, meeting Father here." David tried to cheer himself up with the thought of a good omen.

We were all tired out, ready to drop, sleep for a week, but it was no good Father ordering anyone to bed. We all knew that the time had come, that we had to have it out with Melisande. David went outside again to hold the ponies because I couldn't get through to Dr. Langport at first. When I came out of the shop, he was asleep on his feet.

"Come on, wake up," I said, shaking him. "We've got the ponies to feed and groom before we can even begin to tackle Melisande."

"Couldn't we leave them, just this once?"

"Eleanor would never forgive us. We've got to do our duty by the ponies. She would, even if she were at death's door."

"But she is—that's exactly where she is," David said tearfully.

"Nonsense!" I told him firmly, though I was feeling anything but firm. "We won't think about that until Father comes back from the hospital. We'll hope for the best."

"You sound just like Mother when she knows it's bound to be the worst," David grumbled.

We didn't speak to each other while we rode up to the

stables. It was as much as we could do to keep in the saddle. Peter was there and had practically finished feeding and grooming Bismarck. We offered to let David go back to the barn, but he said he'd rather collapse with exhaustion than be on his own with Melisande.

"Have you seen her?" he asked Peter.

"Seen Melisande?" he echoed. "No. I haven't had time. After telling Mother, I came straight up here."

We worked in silence for a little while, and then Peter said: "Mother realizes we won't feel like eating. She's put hot-water bottles in all our beds, and we're just to have hot drinks and snuggle down in the blankets. A good night's sleep will solve everything, of course."

"Will Mother be required to stay with Mrs. Ridley-Ward?"

"No," said Peter.

David grinned like a simpleton in his relief.

"She said she wouldn't be long," Peter continued, "because the others would come back to the Hall as soon as Father arrived on the scene of the accident."

"Accident!" David exclaimed with feeling.

"Mother thinks Miss Pelham will stay the night with Mrs. Ridley-Ward."

"In case there's any bad news?" David asked.

We didn't need to answer. After another long silence, Peter said: "Mother's a bit worried about Melisande, as a matter of fact."

"She's guessed?" David asked quickly, too quickly.

"No, no such luck," Peter admitted.

"It's no use looking for protection," I told them both angrily. "It's up to us entirely now."

"Why is she worried about Melisande?" David asked.

"She's been white and trembling all the afternoon. She hasn't spoken a word to Mother. She's been lying on her bed, staring into space, for hours. We've got to go straight to sleep, not talk at all. If we're back before Mother, we're not to wait but have our drinks and go to bed."

The thought of bed made my eyes close without any help from me. David began to yawn and yawn and yawn. In a minute, Peter and I were yawning, too.

"We've got to keep awake," I said. "We've got to talk to Melisande. It's a good thing we know they can't hear us downstairs."

"There's another good thing, too," Peter said. "We're to have a night light because of Melisande."

I realized then that Peter was as frightened as David. I knew that whatever I felt (and, after all, I'd seen Eleanor lying there as if she were dead, too), I'd have to seem more than ever like Father. I mustn't lose my head or my temper or my courage. Father never gets angry in a real crisis and always seems to think of the right thing to do. Just when I was thinking that the sooner we faced up to Melisande the better, David said he could hear horses in the distance.

"That means Father's found them," Peter said.

"It means Mother will be back to the barn soon," David said.

"It won't make any difference whether she's there or

not," I told him. "We're on our own with Melisande more than ever now. Imagine what would happen if we started talking about spells and witches tonight. Mother would say the shock had been too much for us, and Father would give us medicine to make us go to sleep, and that would be the end of everything."

"The end of Eleanor, anyway," said Peter. Nothing seems to stop him making dreadful jokes, but it was a good sign. It showed he was beginning to face up to Melisande too, in his own way.

"If Father says she's still alive when he gets back, that means tonight's our last chance," I said.

It was what we'd all been thinking ever since we left Eleanor unconscious on the ground, but we hadn't dared to say it. Now that I'd put it into words, we were none of us so afraid.

9

THE CRISIS

We finished quickly now and hurried back to the barn, our brave resolutions filling us with fresh energy. The lights were on, and Mother had lit a fire. The barn looked cozy and inviting, and we would have been comforted by the faint glow of the night light coming from our loft window if we had not known that Melisande was waiting there. Mother came in while I was making the hot chocolate.

"No news yet. Father's just telephoned to say he's on his way back from the hospital and that Eleanor is still unconscious. Miss Pelham's back, and she says that Sultan is behaving very oddly. She's sure he deliberately threw Eleanor—a thing that's never happened before. She's taking him to the pony-club stables to be looked after, and then she's coming back to stay the night with Mrs. Ridley-Ward. Father expects to find you all in bed, so don't be long."

Mother called out to Melisande, but she didn't answer. She had to shout loudly to make herself heard up in our loft, even when the curtain wasn't drawn across the partition. She went into the kitchen and stood at the bottom of the ladder.

"Hot chocolate and hot buttered toast made at the fire," she called out temptingly. But there was no reply.

"Perhaps she's asleep," I suggested.

"Go up quietly then, but if she isn't asleep, don't tell her any gory details. You can take another night light for your end, just this once."

Mother lit the night light and put it in a saucer.

"I've put on an extra blanket, and your beds will be nice and warm," she said, handing me the light. "You'll be asleep in two shakes of a lamb's tail."

"Wonder what we'd be in two shakes of Sultan's tail?" Peter whispered, as we obediently trooped quietly through the kitchen.

"Good night," said Mother, "and put the light well away from your bed. It's dangerous up there."

"Famous last words again," Peter muttered, and I knew he would do his best now to keep our spirits up.

"Good night," we murmured as we began to climb the ladder.

When we were all perched on it, in a line, we heard the car coming up the lane, and Mother ran out to meet it. We all stayed where we were, in a row on the ladder, and listened. In her haste, Mother had left the barn door open, and we heard the car stop and Father get out of it, and we heard them talking, but we couldn't make out what they said. Peter volunteered to creep back into the room, to see if he could hear, but there was no need. They came back to the door of the barn, and though they didn't come in, we could just make out their conversation.

"I promised I'd go up and see if there was anything I could do for Mrs. Ridley-Ward," Father said.

"She's having hysterics," Mother replied, "making the most of it."

"Won't be easy to quiet her down," said Father. "I've nothing definite I can tell her—unfortunately. Very queer case altogether. No internal injury or fracture as far as we can tell. These states of coma do happen sometimes after bad falls. Nothing to do but wait. Mr. Ridley-Ward's staying the night with Dr. Langport in the town."

"Is there anything else we can do?" asked Mother.

"I'll tell Mrs. Ridley-Ward to send a message over if anything happens in the night, and I'll drive her into the town, if necessary. Miss Pelham ought to have a rest. I'd better get this over, and we'll try to get some sleep ourselves in case I have to turn out."

Their voices grew fainter as they walked back to the car.

"Children all right? D'you think they need a sedative?"

I resisted the temptation to say: "I told you so."

"They're asleep already, I shouldn't wonder," Mother answered. "Bed's the best treatment for shock."

"Mr. Ridley-Ward said they behaved splendidly. He seemed to be in rather a shocked condition himself. Judith showed great presence of mind," he said.

As we clambered into the loft, I made a vow to live up to my reputation, whatever was in store for us. We heard Mother come back into the barn. She blew up the fire with the bellows, and then she drew the heavy curtain across the partition.

We were cut off. We couldn't hear them, and they couldn't hear us. We were on our own with Melisande. As an extra precaution, Peter covered the ladder hole with a blanket. I set down the night light by my bed. Then we all looked at Melisande.

She was still dressed, lying flat on her back like an effigy on a tombstone, with something clasped in her hands. Haunched on her pillow, like an Egyptian statue, was the cat.

I picked up the night light and walked toward her. Peter and David came with me. Our shadows on the wall seemed almost comforting when we looked at Melisande and thought of how we had last seen Eleanor.

I bent forward to see what Melisande was holding and, as I did so, Peter gasped.

Clutched tightly between her fingers was a copy of the plait that had been tangled in Sultan's tail. There were the same evil plants—deadly nightshade, ivy, bittersweet, white bryony and black bryony. I grabbed hold of it and gave a great tug. Melisande sat up, and there was the plait in my hand.

"Throw it away!" she cried.

I tried not to show my surprise. I gave the plait to Peter, and he hurled it from the window. The cat sprang from the pillow and hid in the shadows of the loft. Whatever we'd expected, it hadn't been this.

Melisande was *glad* to see us; that was clear. I put our light on the box by hers so that there was a double glow. We each wrapped ourselves in a blanket and cuddled our hot-water bottles and sat around her bed. I gave her my bot-

tle because her hands were like ice. We waited to see what
she would do next.

"Is she dead?" she asked.

"No. She's unconscious, though."

"Did Mother tell you?" David asked. "She told us not
to say anything."

"No need to tell me," Melisande answered impatiently.

"If you could do it, then why can't you undo it?" Peter
asked.

"You know what I am—or half of me." Melisande sighed,
a mournful, melancholy sigh. "If you don't think of a way
to save Eleanor, you won't save my ordinary self," she
threatened. "I'll be evil for the rest of my life, entirely evil

all the time, not merely wicked now and then. And you'll have to grow up with me."

"Why didn't you say this before, straight out?" Peter demanded. "You haven't left us much time."

"I've often tried," said Melisande, "but you've all been such cowards. I had to wait until you were all brave."

"At least a part of Melisande is on our side then?" I asked hopefully.

"Let's hope it's the ordinary part!" exclaimed Peter.

"When did it begin, your being two different halves united in one person?" David asked.

"I've been like it ever since I was born," Melisande replied gloomily, "and I'd hardly call it 'united.' I've never felt like a whole person, like an ordinary girl. I'm not even exactly half of one thing and half of another. Sometimes I feel three-quarters Montgomery and only a quarter of the other one. Sometimes it's the other way around. It was the other way around when I wove the deadly plait and wished Eleanor harm. I was three-quarters the other one then."

"More like ninety-nine hundredths," said Peter, "and only a hundredth of ordinary girl, the curse is working so well."

"If it succeeds, I'll lose even that tiny bit of Montgomery. If Eleanor dies, I'll lose it forever"—and Melisande burst into tears. It was the first time she'd ever cried, but when I tried to comfort her, she pushed me away.

"Don't try to stop me," she begged. "It shows there's a bit of me left that's human. That's my Montgomery bit, fighting back."

"Montgomery!" Peter shouted—so loudly that we all sat

absolutely silent for a moment, thinking Mother must have heard down below. Peter was bursting to explain himself.

"D'you notice she keeps saying Montgomery when she talks about her ordinary self? Montgomery, *not* Melisande. All we've got to do is change her name."

Melisande shook her head. "It's got to come from inside," she said. "It's got to belong to me; I've got to feel it's part of me. I've got to be more Montgomery, all Montgomery, not something quite different. We've got to use what's there already unless you can think of the right countercharm for Eleanor."

"If you can't think of it, I don't see how we can," David complained.

"The magic part of me's only black magic. Haven't you realized that yet?" Melisande replied furiously.

"And that part of you, the angry-at-our-stupidity part, is pure Montgomery," Peter pointed out. "I'm sure I'm right. I refuse to give up. What's your second name?"

"I haven't got one. Melisande Montgomery's enough for one child."

"More than enough for half a child," Peter declared.

"Are you absolutely certain?" David asked. "The rest of us have a second name. I'm David John."

"I'm Peter George."

"And I'm Judith Mary."

"If I had a second name," said Melisande, and she was becoming more and more melancholy, "it'd be something like Circe, and that would only make matters worse."

"I can think of a good few people I'd like changed into swine," was Peter's comment.

"If you want to convince us that your idea is a serious one," I told him, "you're going the wrong way about it."

"It's the only idea anyone's had," Peter retorted. "Supposing you go and ask Mother if Melisande's got a second name? You've just got time before Father comes back."

"If you're going to do anything, you'll have to make haste," Melisande pointed out. "After midnight, the other one will be more powerful than ever."

"You come with me then," I told Melisande. "If Mother thinks it's one of your whims, she'll be patient with us."

Peter moved the blanket from the ladder hole, and I took one of the night lights and we climbed down. Peter and David followed—they were going to listen from behind the curtain.

Mother was sitting by the fire. She wasn't doing anything, which was unusual for her. We startled her, coming into the room when she imagined us fast asleep in the loft.

"It's Melisande," I stuttered, keeping a weather eye on the door and an ear cocked for Father's return. This wasn't the sort of nonsense he'd tolerate tonight of all nights. "She's had a nightmare." I was suddenly inspired. "She says there's a giant who wants to know her second name before he'll let her go free. Has she got a second name?"

Mother looked at me suspiciously and looked at the curtain. I'd heard Peter's stifled gasp of admiration at my inventiveness on the spur of the moment, but I hoped Mother hadn't. Fortunately, she was very much in the mood of "anything for a quiet life."

"Of course she's got a second name. You all have. Peter John, David George. Or is it David John and Peter George? One or the other. And you're Judith Mary. And Melisande . . . oh dear! I can't remember."

David came rushing out from behind the curtain.

"It's a matter of life and death!"

Mother looked at him rather oddly, and then she said, "You might as well come and join us by the fire, Peter," and we knew she was going to humor us. I suppose she thought this was our way of reacting to the shock we'd had—being very childish. We hoped Father would think so, too, if he came in and found us all out of bed, asking silly questions.

"It was only one syllable," said Mother, after thinking very hard, "because she had seven already."

"Seven!" Peter cried. "A magic number. You remember the stable door, Judith?"

"That was German measles," I replied, without thinking. "This is quite a different case."

"I should think it is," Mother observed. "Two cases of something on the brain. Are you feeling all right?"

"Yes, yes," Peter answered impatiently. "It's a code. Don't worry about us."

"Think hard," I begged her. "We'll all think hard in words of one syllable."

"David will find that difficult," Peter joked, but we made him be quiet.

"Is it June?"

"Or May?"

"No, no, not a month."

"Is it Rose?"

"No, not a flower."

"Jane?"

"Jill?"

"It wasn't an ordinary name like that."

"It *isn't* a name like that, you should say." Peter rebuked her. "It still *is* Melisande's second name, if only we can think of it. Is it Pearl?"

"Or Dawn?"

"No, no. It doesn't describe anything. It wasn't—isn't— anything real."

"There you are!" said Melisande. "I told you so!"

"Mother means not animal, vegetable, or mineral," David explained.

"That's it," said Mother. "Twenty questions."

"Abstract," David elaborated, and we knew he must be feeling happier.

"That's right; that's the word," said Mother.

"Faith?"

"Hope?"

"Grace?"

Mother shook her head. "It's no good. It's quite gone. Couldn't you pretend to the giant?" she asked Melisande.

"He'd know," Melisande replied. "In any case," she added quite suddenly, as if she'd just made up her mind, "I want to be called by my second name from tonight. I shall wait and ask Father what it is if you can't remember."

Mother began to get ruffled.

"I'll ask him in the morning myself. I promise. I don't think tonight would be a very good time."

"It's the only time," Melisande answered.

"Oh dear." Mother looked at her sadly. "Where are the pains? What's it to be this time?"

"There's nothing the matter with me," said Melisande, "but the other one . . ."

"She means the giant," I interrupted hastily. Father might still decide to give us all a sleeping tablet. "The giant won't wait until morning. She's more afraid of the giant than Father."

"We'll go back to bed," said Peter, "and leave Melisande here. Father won't mind so much if we're not all here."

I picked up our night light again, and Mother stared into the fire, desperately trying to think of the name so that she could send Melisande to bed with us.

"Fay? No. Gay? No," she mumbled to herself. "Gay? Gay?" Suddenly she stood up and cried: "Joy! That's it. How silly of me to forget. Joy!"

Peter began to hop, skip, and jump around the room crying: "Joy, oh joy! Joy of my life, oh joy!" and Melisande clapped her hands, and David laughed overloudly because he was overexcited, so that we didn't hear Father come until he was in the room, stamping his foot and shouting: "I won't have it."

We'd never seen him really angry with Mother before. It was the nearest they ever got to quarreling in front of us.

"What can you be thinking of?" Father said. "Letting them rampage about after the shock they've had. Asking for trouble, in their fatigued condition. Have you no sense at all, woman?"

Never in our lives before had we heard Father calling Mother "woman," and we hoped we never would again. We stood there speechless while Mother made no attempt to explain or defend herself. This made Father wild with rage, but just as he was about to explode, Melisande tugged at his jacket. He looked down at her.

"It's my fault. I wanted to know my second name. It's Joy. Joy Montgomery. You're to call me that."

It was Father's turn to be speechless now, but he soon recovered.

"You're a selfish, thoughtless little girl," he said, "whatever you're called."

Then we remembered Eleanor. We remembered why we were all here asking Mother Melisande's second name. We looked at her, hoping she really was a little girl, but to us she still looked like the other one. She was Melisande and she was responsible for Eleanor's fall and Eleanor might die. We knew she remembered all this too. She shrank away from us all and slunk from the room.

"She's had a miserable day," said Mother.

Father forgot his rage in an instant. He took my night light, drew back the curtain, and said he'd come and tuck us all in.

"Is there any news of Eleanor?" Mother asked.

"Dr. Langport telephoned just as I left the Hall to say there was no change."

We turned to follow Melisande, and Father held up the night light while we climbed the ladder. Melisande had easily found her way in the dark.

We'd hardly gotten to the top when there was a fierce knocking on the door of the barn. Father shoved the night light into the ladder hole and nearly fell off the bottom rungs in his haste to get to the door. He didn't stop to see us crowding back to listen. We heard Miss Pelham's voice. She sounded terribly out of breath.

"I've run all the way," she gasped. Thank goodness she always shouted. "They've just this minute telephoned. Eleanor's come around! I knew you'd want to know. Just for a minute, Dr. Langport says, and she didn't recognize anyone, but she was quite definitely conscious. He says there's hope."

10

THE CURE

We tumbled each other up into the loft like a litter of pigs at play, and I flung the blanket over the ladder hole. Immediately Peter shouted jubilantly: "Oh joy, oh joy of my life, oh joy!"

"Shut up for a minute," I warned him, "until Mother draws the curtain."

We waited until we heard the door slam and footsteps fade and the swish and thud of the curtain falling into place.

"I'm a genius!" Peter did a war dance of triumph. "As long as we all keep calling her Joy, it will be all right."

Melisande-Joy shook her head.

"It's not *all* right—it's only a little right," she complained. "We haven't got rid of Melisande as easily as that. There's something else you've got to do. The Joy part of me will help you as much as it can, but the nearer it gets to midnight, the less of Joy there'll be."

Peter was subdued. He sat on the floor by Melisande-Joy's bed, and David sat beside him. I looked out of the window. There was no streak of light shining out to the gate, so I could tell Mother and Father had gone quickly to bed. Miss Pelham's news must have made them forget about us, and I suppose they believed we were asleep. The moon was coming up, and the countryside was still, peaceful, and empty. Everything looked new and untouched. I could see the church and the rectory across the field, a black shape and a white shape.

I turned away from the window. Melisande-Joy was explaining something very intently to Peter and David.

"I want to be all Joy, but there doesn't seem to be room. We'll have to drive the other one out before the ordinary one can take possession. They're having a fearful tussle at the moment."

"Is it like indigestion?" David asked.

"It's not like any ordinary pain, and I've had enough of those to be able to tell," she said. "It's not like anything Father could cure."

"What we need is a witch doctor, not a family doctor," said Peter.

"I know what it's called," David said excitedly. "Melisande's got to be exorcized. That's what it's called when witch doctors summon forth evil spirits and cure people of the devil."

"As there aren't any witch doctors available, just at present," said Peter scathingly, "we'll have to do it ourselves."

"But we don't know how," said David, trying to back out and wishing he hadn't thought of the right word.

"So far we've done the right thing without knowing how," Peter pointed out. "I don't think you have to be a properly qualified witch doctor. I believe there's something in the Prayer Book about it—I'm sure there's a special service for delivering young sisters from resident demons."

"Of course you ought to know," David retorted sarcastically. "You're very familiar with the contents of the Prayer Book."

"If we weren't such heathens, we'd have one here and we could look it up," I interrupted.

"We could go to the church," said Melisande-Joy.

Peter gazed at her in admiration.

"That's really a sound idea," he said.

David gazed at her in horror.

"It'll be locked," he said, hoping it would be.

"Only in the summer months," said Melisande-Joy, "when the church isn't used every Sunday. When Mr. Cricklemore's on duty, it's always open, so that tramps can go in, if they like, on a cold night."

"Might be one there tonight," said David fearfully.

"Hallowed ground!" exclaimed Peter. "The very thing! We needn't bother about a proper service. Melisande will turn tail as soon as we set foot over the threshold, and Joy can pop into her place."

"Supposing Father catches us?" asked David.

"I'll make sure they're asleep," said Melisande-Joy. "I can move without being heard. I might as well make use of Melisande while I've got her. We can creep out one at a time. The moon's up."

Before I had time to make up my mind to take the risk, she had gone, and in a flash she was back.

"They're snoring," she announced. "Let's go. We're all dressed."

We looked at each other in astonishment.

"I wonder Mother didn't notice when I pretended you'd had a nightmare," I said.

"I've felt all the time that there's been a ray of hope," Peter insisted. "Father didn't notice either."

"That was the heat of the moment, not a ray of hope," David objected, but Peter ignored him.

"I'm sure we're doing the right thing. I feel inspired."

"I don't," said Melisande-Joy lugubriously. "It's Melisande who has the inspirations. Joy has practical ideas. Between the two of them, I don't know where I am. I'll have to depend on you."

"On Montgomery," Peter agreed.

"I'll go first," said Melisande-Joy, preparing to climb down the ladder. "I'll wait by the gate, behind the hedge."

"But *we* can't go through the room and open and shut the door without being heard or seen," David protested. "We're not magicians, not even half of us."

"The kitchen window, stupid," she replied. "I'll leave it wide open, prop it up, so that we can get back without any trouble."

"If ever we do get back," said David pessimistically.

Melisande-Joy disappeared down the ladder in a second. I was ready to follow, but Peter made me wait.

"A minute between each escape," he said. "Otherwise we'll all be caught together."

David followed me, and Peter came last. Waiting for him seemed more like an hour than a minute, and the moment he joined us the moon went behind a cloud.

"That's odd," he said. "It looked like a clear night."

"There goes your ray of hope," I said. I didn't mean to be discouraging, but somehow, now that we were all out in the dark lane, it didn't seem such a stupendous idea. We felt our way to the gap in the hedge, where the footpath to the church began. Suddenly Melisande-Joy stopped and said: "Don't despair, Judith; there is a ray of hope. I can't see in the dark, as usual. Something must be happening to Melisande."

"I'm right, I know I'm right." Peter supported her. "And I've just thought of another good sign. The cat hasn't come. It hasn't been seen since I threw away the plait."

We all looked around, half expecting it to appear at this challenge, but there was no sign of it, and that gave us the courage to go on. We thought it would be easy to keep to the footpath by the feel of it, but there was a frost that night, and all the field was hard and stubbly under our feet.

"Let's feel our way round by the hedge," Peter directed. "It'll be quicker in the end, and we'll have some cover."

We began to stumble in single file around the edge of the field. I thought of Eleanor and why we were here. Melisande-Joy had come up beside me, and she didn't look as if there was much of Joy at home. Her lank hair was blowing about her, her hands and cheeks were about ten degrees colder than mine, and she looked like the Gorgon's head that turned people to stone. An owl flew out of the hedge, hooting.

"Let's go back," pleaded David, coming up on my other side. I gripped his hand tightly, and Peter chanted: "Was there a man dismayed, forward the three and a half Montgomerys."

The owl disappeared into a cloud.

"We'll be safe enough once we get into the churchyard, among the yew trees and tombstones." Peter tried to sound cheerful, but David pressed close to me. "Melisande will feel quite at home there," Peter continued. "It will lull her into a false sense of security, and she won't realize we're making for the church."

"If Joy knows that's where we're going, then Melisande must know as well," David objected.

"You'll give yourself a headache if you go on like that," Peter warned him.

As we passed the rectory, a bat flew out of the garden, circled around Melisande-Joy, and flew back again. She stopped, disheartened.

"Owls and bats, they'll be my only companions," she moaned.

David refused to go on, I felt like giving up, and even Peter was silent. Deep in our dismal thoughts, not one of us noticed a light moving across the field. Shatteringly as a roll of thunder out of a clear sky, we were haloed in the beam of a giant torch, and a voice said: "Well, I never!

Goodness gracious me! Bless my heart and soul! Whatever next!"

I felt only relief that it wasn't Father. Melisande-Joy clapped her hands together and cried: "A light! A light!"

"Pity you didn't notice it sooner," said Peter acidly. "Now we're in for it."

"I didn't mean that sort of light," she replied. She turned to me. "Tell him, tell him everything," she insisted. "Tell him from the very beginning. He'll know what to do."

She flung herself at the little old man and nearly knocked him over.

"Steady now, my dear," he said, holding her off. "Easy does it."

He rubbed his elbows and knees vigorously.

"Cold night, bad for the joints. I'll suffer for it. I can feel a twinge already. But that's a mere nothing. You know about the accident?"

"We were there."

"Fox hunting? Well, well, fancy that. I am surprised. Thought your father knew better. However, that's neither here nor there. I've just been up to see the poor mother; I don't usually keep such late hours. There's a ray of hope, she says, a ray of hope."

"It's you," Melisande-Joy cried. "You're the ray of hope."

"Bless my soul," said Old Sycamore, "whatever is the child talking about? What's going on here? What in the name of goodness are you doing meandering all over my field in the middle of the night?"

"In the name of goodness," Melisande-Joy answered solemnly, "we're going to church," and she began to walk on toward the lich gate. Old Sycamore didn't hesitate. He walked after her, and we walked with him.

"Better tell me about it. Confession is good for the soul."

That was enough to put anyone off, and for a moment I didn't know how to begin.

"Make haste; come along," he said. "And no frills, mind. My old bones want to get warm."

That was better; that was exactly how I could tell him, briefly and quickly, and he listened without interrupting. They didn't sound very much like facts when I put them into words—the things that had made us afraid. I was glad to be telling a grownup at last, though I suppose Old Sycamore wasn't behaving like one. Anyone else would have marched us back to the barn and handed us over to Father. When we got to the church porch, he made us all sit down.

"So you're a witch," he said to Melisande-Joy.

"On and off," she replied, "and it's more on than off at the moment."

Old Sycamore looked at his watch.

"If we don't hurry up, it will be altogether on," he remarked.

"I knew you'd understand." Melisande-Joy almost sighed a human sigh of relief.

"Stranger things have happened," Old Sycamore said. "In this parish, too. I even went to a wise woman myself to have my warts cured when I was a boy. I had to peel a hazel twig at full moon and bury it and then dig it up at the next full moon and my warts would vanish. They did, too. Stranger things, all true. Happening all the time. Everywhere." He was talking to himself now, and I could see what Eleanor meant about his sermons. He spoke again to Melisande-Joy. He wasn't taking much notice of us.

"This is the worst you've ever done. This is really evil," he told her.

We were all silent, and in the silence, we heard the owl hoot, as loudly as if it were on the porch with us.

"Drat and bother," said Old Sycamore. "I thought I might make both of you ashamed, you and the other one. I see it's not going to be as easy as that. You've muddled things up, you know. You've mixed up your magic with some real human hate. That's why it's turned out so badly. Oh, you have made a muddle, you silly old witch, you silly little girl."

Melisande, or I suppose Joy, hung her head. The Montgomery part of her was ashamed all right, but the owl went on hooting. David said it sounded more like laughing, like the demon king's laugh in pantomine, but Old Sycamore told him not to be fanciful.

"Quite enough to get on with without you imagining things," he told David. "Quite enough."

He stood up. "Can't sit here much longer or I'll get stuck. Come along inside, and we'll see what we can do. Don't hang about now, don't lag."

We followed him through the church door.

"Must preach my sermon tomorrow," he was muttering to

himself. "Can't miss my Sunday. Mrs. Griffin will have to make me a mustard bath. Suppose you don't know a spell to cure rheumatism?" he asked Melisande-Joy.

"I don't know any good spells," she replied.

"The first one was a good one," said David. "Incomparable."

"Oh, yes, beautiful spell, quite unique," said Old Sycamore. "Killing off your mother so you could live in the country. A very good spell."

"I didn't mean to," Melisande-Joy explained. "It all got mixed up."

"What a muddle, what a muddle, mixing up real human greed with magic. Silly old witch, silly little girl!"

We were standing by the font, and the moon came out and shone through the windows. Old Sycamore walked up the aisle, through the path of moonlight to the altar, and beckoned us to follow him.

"All kneel down," he said, "anywhere, in the aisle, just there, where you are. Hurry up now."

It was very cold in the church, colder still kneeling down on the stone. Old Sycamore didn't kneel with us. He swung his arms across his chest and blew on his fingers.

"If I get down, I'll never get up again," he said. "Now, shut your eyes."

We obeyed. There was a short silence while we waited for the incantation to begin, but nothing happened.

Suddenly he said: "I suppose you've all been christened?"

We all opened our eyes, and Melisande-Joy stood up.

"I know your poor father's got some unfortunate ideas," continued Old Sycamore. "Had a very interesting chat with him once. That was before the misunderstanding about Snowy." He turned to Melisande-Joy. "That was a near thing, you know. She nearly got you then, the other one. She's very cunning. She knew I'd be *her* enemy as a matter of course and that her only chance was to make me a Montgomery enemy. Very clever, very close shave."

"But if you knew all that," David was bold enough to ask, "why didn't you come and see us any more?"

"Not so much righteous indignation if you please," Old Sycamore replied. "You surely didn't think I believed that awful story Mrs. Griffin spread about?"

"But why didn't you stop her if you knew the truth?" Peter asked.

Melisande-Joy and Old Sycamore exchanged a look that plainly said how stupid we were.

"It was the other one. Don't you understand yet?" Melisande-Joy explained. "She can easily manage people like Mother and Father and Mrs. Griffin—down to earth, common-sense, reasonable people. Don't you remember how I struggled on the night Snowy died? I knew I had to go then. I was nearly all ordinary girl that night, and I might have vanquished the other one if you had helped."

"We weren't afraid that night," Peter protested.

"I was," David admitted.

"We missed that opportunity," I interrupted excitedly,

"so the rector had to wait until we came to him. It had to be purely and simply a Montgomery effort."

"Ah!" said Old Sycamore to Melisande-Joy. "They begin to see the light at last. But this won't do: time's getting on. Now, about this christening."

"The others have been christened, but not me," said Melisande-Joy. "They've all got godparents who send them presents. I haven't."

Old Sycamore sighed. "That's a fine reason for being sure, a very fine reason," he muttered. "Might have guessed; just what I expected. I'll have to have another chat with your poor father."

"Will it make any difference?" David asked. "If she ought to be christened, couldn't you do it now?"

"It would take more than that to make a difference now," replied Old Sycamore. "It would have saved a lot of trouble then, when she was born."

"Mother wanted her to be christened," I said. "Mother hasn't got any unfortunate ideas, but it kept having to be put off, and in the end she was never done."

"Done!" exclaimed the rector. "Done! That's a fine way to describe a christening, a fine way. Dear me, the children of today . . ."

He muttered to himself for a few moments and then he said: "Mr. Ridley-Ward should have known better—new place to live in and no elderbush planted. Must have an elderbush to keep witches out of the house—he should have known that. He's paying for it now, poor man. You must tell your mother to do something about it."

"It's too late," wailed Melisande-Joy. "If you don't stop chattering, it will be too late forever."

"You're quite right. Allow me to apologize. I won't waste any more time. What's going to happen if your parents wake up, I'd like to know, and find out the birds have flown?"

"Miss Pelham might go to the barn with a message," David suggested.

"No, she won't." Melisande-Joy was very positive. "There won't be any change for Eleanor either way until I know whether I'm to be Montgomery or the other one for always."

"She's quite right, once again, quite right. We'd better get on with it. Kneel down and stay there. All this bobbing up and down won't get us anywhere."

We composed ourselves for the second time, eyes tightly shut, hands folded together. There was another short silence and then Old Sycamore said:

"That reminds me, this is strictly between ourselves, of course. Can't have people accusing me of witch-doctoring at my time of life, wouldn't do at all. Have the bishop down on me in no time. That quite clear? I don't need to make you promise? I can trust you?"

"We're all right," Peter answered. "The other one will only be able to behave like a Montgomery if you're a good witch doctor."

"Don't frighten me, young man; don't make me nervous.

I'm well aware of it." Old Sycamore began to get agitated. "I've not had much practice."

"You'll manage. I'm sure you'll manage." I encouraged him.

"We'll see," said the old man, "we'll see soon enough. Now, are we all ready?"

We closed our eyes for the third time.

"Say after me, one at a time, 'Please, God, save Eleanor.' You first, Judith."

It seemed too simple, but perhaps it was only a beginning. I spoke up clearly, and Old Sycamore said: "Good, good. Might have been saying prayers all your life, instead of being the daughter of a heathen."

"Father's not a heathen," I protested. "He's a scientist."

"Same thing, don't argue," he replied irascibly. "Don't waste time. Peter's turn now."

Peter was self-conscious and mumbled, but when he got to the end, he suddenly added: "I really mean it, you know, God; it's not just a trick to get You on our side."

Old Sycamore rubbed his palms together delightedly.

"Now we're getting somewhere. Come along, David."

David even manages to say his multiplication tables poetically, and he uttered the prayer with great feeling and finished with a solemn "Amen."

"Excellent, excellent!" Old Sycamore was hopping about in excitement. "Now you, what's your name? Medusa? Melusine? Minerva?"

"Joy. Joy is my name," said our young sister in her clear, carrying voice.

"Odd, very odd," muttered Old Sycamore. "I thought it began with an M, some enchantress or other. Joy Montgomery? I ought to be able to remember a simple name like that. You're quite sure?"

"Positive," answered Joy, and then she said in a quite ordinary, rather tearful, little-girl's voice: "Please, God, save Eleanor and me."

There was another short silence, and then Old Sycamore said: "Come along, get up! What are you waiting for?"

"Is that all?" asked David.

"All!" he replied. "I should think it is all. Haven't you had enough for one day? What more d'you want, I'd like to know. Come along, hurry up now. I'll be frozen stiff tomorrow if I don't get home to Mrs. Griffin."

He hobbled down the aisle to the door, and we followed him.

"Off you go," he said. "I'll give you time to get under the hedge. We don't want Mrs. Griffin rushing out to meet me and catching us red-handed. Or should I say blackhanded?"

He held open the heavy door. We heard the church clock chiming midnight.

"Just in time," said Joy.

"Gracious me," said the rector. "I shall get into trouble. Off you go, and, remember, not a word."

We came out onto the porch, first me, then Peter, then

David, and Joy last. I looked back to make sure we were all ready before I made for the lich gate and the shelter of the hedge. I saw Old Sycamore make a sign over Joy as she passed him. So it wasn't all, then, and I wondered what the sign could have been. Joy came up and took my hand and said: "It was the sign of the cross, Judith, and that's the very last time I shall ever be able to read anyone's thoughts."

11

THE PROOF

The moon was very bright now, and all the clouds had
disappeared. We sprinted across the field by the footpath
and didn't stop to breathe until we were through the gap
and up the lane to our gate. We had to stop then—we were
all panting like thirsty dogs—but it was very nearly our
undoing.

"Look out! Someone's coming. I can hear footsteps," Peter
hissed. "Quick, back to the gap in the rectory field."

Fright gave us a second wind. We could all hear footsteps now, someone running, someone going into our field.
We heard the gate creak as it was opened.

"It's Miss Pelham!" cried Joy. "He's done it! I'm saved!"

"Hurrah for Old Sycamore!" cheered Peter.

It didn't occur to any of us that it might be bad news. We
strained our ears to hear if Miss Pelham went into the barn:
it would be our chance to slip back. We heard her knocking on the door, long and loud. We heard the door open,
heard Father's voice, and then the door shut, and there
were no more footsteps coming away. While we listened,
to make sure, the owl hooted, far, far away. Peter waved his
hand in the direction from where it sounded, fainter and
fainter.

"Good-by," he called. "Good-by, Melisande." And then it faded away altogether. We didn't stop to wonder about that. We had to hurry. We rushed around to the side of the barn and shoved each other through the kitchen window. As we crept through the kitchen, we could hear them talking, but we dared not stop to listen. They'd be bound to come and see if we'd been disturbed by the knocking. We scrambled up the ladder and undressed like maniacs. David was struggling with his pajama buttons, his fingers all thumbs he was so nervous, when we heard the curtain being drawn back. I shoved him onto his bed, grabbed the blanket off the floor by the ladderhole, and flung it over him. We could hear Father in the kitchen.

"Lot of scuffling," he said. "We'd better tell them if they're restless. Then they can sleep the sleep of the just."

"Of the just in time, more like it," Peter whispered to me from under his blankets.

"That's mice," Mother said. "They were all dog-tired. It can wait until morning. Good news keeps."

They had climbed the ladder by now and stood in the loft.

"Let's blow out these lights," Father said. "The moon's bright enough. Not even Melisande will wake now."

Mother tiptoed to Joy's bed and took away the night light.

"She's having a pleasant dream for once," Mother said, "actually smiling in her sleep."

While Mother turned her back to my bed to take the

other night light, I opened my eyes for a second. Father was gazing around the loft in astonishment, looking at our clothes scattered all over the place.

"Anyone would think there'd been an alarm," he said.

Mother began to pick up our clothes.

"They feel quite warm," she said, "as though they'd just taken them off."

I shut my eyes very tightly and held my breath. David said afterward he'd clenched his teeth so hard on the blanket that he'd bitten a hole in it. Peter frankly admitted that he'd prayed.

"Quite useful, once you get the hang of it," he said airily.

"Too tired to know what they were doing," Father said. "We won't wake them."

Mother dropped the clothes, and they tiptoed to the ladder hole.

"It's very strange," were the last words I heard her say, "because it's a very cold night."

And then I must have fallen asleep. We all fell asleep, and we didn't wake up the next morning until the church bells were ringing for Old Sycamore's eleven-o'clock service.

" 'Don't you forget. Don't tell a soul.' That's what the bells are saying," David said.

" 'O joyful day, hip hip hooray,' is what I hear," Peter contradicted.

" 'Gone to her doom. Poor Melisande.' That's what comes into my head," Joy confessed.

"I'm not sorry," I replied. "'Let us give thanks. Down with the witch,' is what my chime rings out."

"Are you awake? Time to get up!" Mother came into the kitchen and called to us.

"She's hearing the bells, too," David said, laughing.

"We're getting up now. Just coming," I called back in what I hoped was a voice stricken with woe.

We all came down, looking as forlorn and anxious as we possibly could. Mother had blown up the fire, and there was hot porridge with cream and brown sugar, and in the middle of the table was an autumn nosegay. It was bright and sweet and feathery, very different from Melisande's revolting skein of poisonous plants. Mother and Father had called at the Hall and been for a walk. The nosegay was Mother's work; she'd gotten rather good at that sort of thing since we'd been in the country. Father was sitting by the fire, drinking coffee.

"Come on, lazybones," he said. "We've been up for hours."

"You'll be late for church," Mother said jokingly.

We looked at each other with concern and guilt.

"Should we have gone, d'you think?" Peter asked Joy before he could stop himself.

"Remember what you said," Joy reminded him, "about it not being a trick. If we *wanted* to go, it would be the thing to do, not otherwise."

"No good going just because we think we *ought* to?" Peter asked.

"They won't be taken in," Joy explained, "Old Sycamore and God. You don't want me to have a relapse?"

"What's this?" asked Mother, using her common sense. "Another code, I suppose?"

"Sounds like a reasonable discussion to me," Father replied, "as far as I can get the hang of it. Just what I'm always telling them. No humbug. Exactly what I said to the Reverend Tobias Cricklemore when he asked why we weren't at church."

We grinned at each other, remembering our "poor father's unfortunate ideas," but hastily changed our expressions when we remembered we mustn't look happy.

"It's all right," Mother said. "The funeral's over. Come and have breakfast. You must be ravenous by now."

We certainly were. Father waited while we crammed in the first few mouthfuls of hot, delicious food before he told us what we already knew.

"Eleanor came out of her coma at about midnight and shouted for the night nurse," Father said. "She wanted to know why she was in the hospital and demanded to go home at once, as there was nothing the matter with her, except that she was very hungry."

"Typical!" said Peter, but he said it in an admiring, not a critical, way. I wondered how long he would be able to keep it up.

"The night nurse got into a state," Father continued, "and begged Eleanor to keep quiet while she sent a nurse to fetch Dr. Langport and Mr. Ridley-Ward. Eleanor got very annoyed then, according to Miss Pelham. She said she'd been knocked silly by a fall before and there hadn't been all this hullabaloo. The night nurse explained that she'd been unconscious for some time. 'Well, I'm not unconscious now,' Eleanor said, 'so get me something to eat.' "

"That's what I call a rapid recovery," said Mother.

"What did the night nurse do?" I asked.

"She said Eleanor must wait. Then Eleanor got rather peeved, Miss Pelham says, and told the nurse that her father was one of the hospital governors and that he'd given the hospital a lot of money and that if the nurse didn't get some grub at once, Eleanor would get her father to make a complaint."

"Miss Pelham was tickled to death by that, of course," Mother interrupted. " 'That's my Eleanor,' she said."

"Then Eleanor hasn't changed?" David asked, very puzzled.

Father roared with laughter. "She's only recovered, I'm afraid. Isn't that enough for you? Or were you expecting a miracle?"

That made Joy laugh. I gave her a warning nudge, because Mother looked at her, obviously remembering the state she—or rather, Melisande—had been in yesterday afternoon. However, all Mother said, after watching Joy laughing herself silly, was: "D'you know, I think we might have that brace off your teeth now. I don't think you need it any more."

Then Father looked at Joy. "I believe you're right," he said.

Joy took the ugly brace off her teeth and went to the door and flung it out as far as she could. She came back to the table, grinning from ear to ear.

"Quite an improvement," Father admitted. "Child looks almost human."

That started Peter off. He choked into his third helping of porridge, and tears streamed into his plate. Mother and Father were beginning to exchange glances, so I quickly started to ask questions—common-sense, reasonable questions.

"Are they going to let Eleanor come home?"

"She's there already. She got so furious when they wanted to keep her in the hospital under observation that Dr. Langport decided she'd be better off at home with a nurse. They managed to get hold of one right away to come back to the Hall this morning with Eleanor and her father. Eleanor's promised to be good and stay in bed and do as she's told until they're certain there's no hidden injury."

"Did Dr. Langport say if they'd discovered the cause?"

"It's got us all floored. These things do happen occasionally, and very worrying they are, too. All that Eleanor seems to be worried about is the ponies, of course. Miss Pelham's promised to look after them until she's fit to be up and about again. Apparently Sultan is as tranquil as an ox this morning."

"Doesn't seem to have affected her nerve," Mother observed. "Plucky girl, I will say that for her. Can't wait to go riding again. Quite fearless."

"You sound like Miss Pelham," Father said, laughing. Then: "What about you?" he asked us suddenly. "You had a bad fright."

"I should think we did," said David, and then he and Peter and Joy all began to laugh helplessly again.

"They seem to have gotten over it," Mother remarked, "and in any case there won't be any riding until Eleanor's better."

"Had we better go up to the house, just to say how glad we are to hear the news?" I suggested, trying very hard to be sensible.

"Very thoughtful," said Father. "Ask to speak to Mrs. Ridley-Ward, but don't go in, don't stay long, and don't talk too much."

We all jumped up from the table, anxious to rush off. We knew we had to put Joy Montgomery to the test of the outside world. Mother and Father were no good—if they had noticed any difference, they'd only have thought their patience and understanding had been rewarded.

But Mother called us back.

"You'd better make yourselves look presentable," she said. "You look as if you'd been out all night.'"

This time I found it difficult not to smile myself.

"In that case," said Peter, "you'll have to plait Joy's hair. That's the only way she's fit to be seen by Eleanor's mother."

"Joy?" said Father. "Who the d . . ."

"Don't say it!" I cried.

"Good heavens . . ." Mother began.

"That's better," said Joy.

"You seem to be better, too," Mother said. "Quite recovered. Last night I thought . . ."

"Last night you promised . . ." Joy interrupted her.

"Promised to call her Joy," Peter joined in. "Don't you remember? Allow me to introduce you to Joy Montgomery."

Father solemnly shook hands with his youngest child.

"It certainly sounds better," he said. "The question is—does it suit her?"

He put his hands on her shoulders and eyed her seriously.

"Sit down," he said. "Over here, away from the table."

We all gathered around. It was an important moment. We hadn't thought what would happen if Father wouldn't have Joy.

"Get a towel, one of you," Father said. "And Mother's scissors."

We handed him the things he asked for.

"This seems more like the beginning of an incantation than Old Sycamore's effort," Peter whispered to me.

"Science versus Religion," David muttered back.

"Except that it isn't versus," Peter argued.

Father lifted up Joy's long, straggly black hair.

"Plaiting this is no good," he said. "Look at it, just like a wi . . ."

He didn't have time to say it.

"Rapunzel!" David shouted. "Just like Rapunzel."

"Rapunzel had beautiful long golden hair," Father replied.

"But she was in a witch's power," David said, "just like . . ."

But we all trod on his toes and dug our elbows into him, and he stopped—as he admitted afterward—on the brink of disclosure. Father was, as usual, absorbed in the job in hand, and Mother was still in her "deaf ear and blind eye" mood.

"I'm going to cut off all this," Father announced.

"Just long enough to cover her ears; that's what it needs." Mother agreed.

Father held up a lock of hair, looked at Joy's ears, and held the scissors in mid-air.

"They used to be pointed ears," he said, "very pointed."

"So they did." Mother agreed.

"Very strange," said Father. "They've certainly changed. It's an improvement, anyway." And he got on with the cutting. Soon there was a pile of lank ends on the floor, and with every snip of the scissors Joy looked more like Joy than ever.

"There we are! Done!" said Father proudly.

Joy jumped up and shook her head this way and that.

"It's quite thick, with all those rat's-tails cut off," said Mother. "It looks like a bell, the shape of a bell."

Father scooped up the ends and threw them on the fire. They didn't burn. They shot straight up the chimney.

"Where have they gone?" David said, astonished.

"Changed into a flock of black crows, I expect." Peter teased him. "Listen, can't you hear them cawing as they come out of the chimney and fly away? They've gone to join the owl."

"Don't be an idiot," said Mother, for David had rushed to the door to see. "You know very well there are always crows in the field. That's what you can hear, David."

"Crows don't mix with owls, in any case," Father said.

"It might be what I can hear, but it's not what I can see,"

said David, turning solemnly into the room. Then he looked at Joy, bouncing about in front of the mirror, looking at her teeth and patting her hair.

"Take off your spectacles," David said. "You might be able to see as well."

"As well as what?" Father asked sharply. "Enough of this nonsense. Just because she's changed her name and had her hair cut, you're expecting another miracle, I suppose?"

"No, the same one," said Peter, under his breath to me.

"No whispering," said Father, beginning to get angry. "And don't try any experiments while I'm not looking. We don't want any more accidents. You know perfectly well that she's as blind as a bat."

"As a bat," echoed David, staring out of the door.

"If there's any more of this," Mother threatened, "you'll all have an aspirin and go straight back to bed."

"On second thought, I'm not sure that a complete day's rest wouldn't be a good thing for all of you," Father declared. "Perhaps you'd better not go after all."

We knew that we had to go. Was it possible that the other one hadn't absolutely vanished, that we'd nearly wrecked everything by our carelessness? We waited in anguish for Father to make up his mind, not daring to look at Joy. We heard her give a cry of alarm. I looked up to see the cat walk into the room. Then Joy began to smile—a beautiful smile. The cat was purring. It took no notice of her but rubbed itself against Father's legs. Father was so surprised that he forgot everything else.

"Good heavens!" he said, looking down.

Peter suddenly clutched my arm.

"As white as snow, as black as—" he whispered. "As black as what?"

"As soot." David obliged.

Peter poured the remains of the cream into a saucer. He set it down by the fire.

"Sooty, Sooty," he called, and the cat purred even louder and went to the saucer. Peter looked at us triumphantly, and Mother said: "Wonders will never cease!"

We didn't miss this opportunity; we moved to the door. As we went out, Joy picked up the nosegay.

"I'll take this for Eleanor," she said. "May I?" Mother nodded.

When she thought we were clear of the barn, I heard Mother say to Father: "There is something in it, you know. Change the name and change the character."

"You're as bad as the children," Father answered. "Superstitious nonsense!" But—and it was the only time ever—he didn't add: "I won't have it."

As soon as we got a little way down the lane, for we had to go by the road and call at the front door of the house like proper visitors, Joy took off her spectacles. She blinked a bit at first, and we helped her along, but when we got to the gap in the hedge, she suddenly stopped. David was hopping up and down beside her like a jack in the box. She dropped her spectacles and stretched out her hands.

"I can see perfectly clearly," she announced, "plain as can be. I can see the rectory and the hedge and the lich gate and the yew trees and the tombstones. I can see as well as any of you."

"I told you so, I told you so," David cried.

"Father always said it was curious, your being short-sighted," Peter said, remembering. "He couldn't understand why because it didn't run in the Montgomery family."

"If you hadn't made one of your silly remarks, I'd never have seen," David said to Peter.

"Seen what?" we all asked.

"A bat flew out of the chimney when we put *her* hair on the fire. I knew Joy wouldn't be as blind as a bat, whatever the other one was." David was beside himself with pride, with having been the one to see and to understand.

"I don't see how we'll explain that to Father," I said. "There can't be a reasonable or a common-sense explanation. He was suspicious enough about the pointed ears."

David was still jigging up and down.

"It'll have to be a gradual improvement then," Joy said, stooping down to pick up her spectacles and put them on again. But she was too late. David had jumped on them, and they were shattered to smithereens.

"We aren't meant to pretend. Don't you remember," Peter said, as we all looked down at the broken spectacles. "If we take the risk, it will be all right. I've often heard

Father say short-sighted children get better when they stop growing. Perhaps he'll think you've stopped growing."

"I believe I have," said Joy, "upwards at any rate. I feel a lot fatter this morning."

"All that porridge," said Peter. "Come on! Now for the final proof."

We raced each other along the lane, up the road, and down the drive. The nurse opened the door.

"Mr. and Mrs. Ridley-Ward have gone to church," she said, "to offer up a thanksgiving."

Joy gave the nurse the nosegay.

"Will you give this to Eleanor from us," she asked, "with our thanksgiving, I mean our best wishes."

David giggled, and the nurse looked us up and down rather severely.

"What name shall I say?"

"Oh, the Montgomerys," Joy replied, "tell her it's from the Montgomerys."

The nurse took the nosegay.

"I'll tell her," she promised. "From the Montgomerys—all four of them. Good morning."